Zoon Garden

ZOON GARDEN

THE DECLINE OF A NATION

JORDAN O'DONNELL

Tribe Supply

For information regarding permission, write to Jacob Harris at www.jordanodonnellauthor.com/contact

LCCN 2020907409

IBSN 9781734962802 (Paperback)
IBSN 9781734962819 (eBook)
IBSN 9781734962833 (Hardback)
BISAC: Fiction/Satire | Fiction/Political | Fiction/Dystopian

First Edition
1 2 3 4 5 6 7 8 9 10

Edited by David Burton and by Michael Coghlan
Cover Design and Illustration by Phil Poole
Interior Book Design by Patrick Johns

Library of Congress Cataloging-in-Publication Data has been applied for.

To Pura, for food in the belly
To Michael, for shelter over the head
To Tom, for ideas of the mind

If truth be that which sets man free,
the greatest trick the devil shall play is convincing
the world truth does not exist.

1

ISABELLA THE GIRAFFE waited for her routinely punctual handler an additional five minutes before inspecting the gray stone office. Dark circles surrounded her eyes, and she had a way of squinting as though each thing she saw deserved thorough study. She stood on her hoof tips, chin over the fence, brown eyes scanning the land in the west, and muttered, "Where are they?" She turned around to a group of giraffes. "Where are the humans? I don't see a single one anywhere in the zoo."

The other giraffes, some twenty in total, stretched their necks over the fence and peered both ways down the asphalt path. Isabella's mate, a giraffe named Sharif, lowered his chin from the fence. "I don't see those two-legged walkers anywhere," he said. A sly smile flickered across his face. "Bella, this might be the day."

"Rubbish," said Isabella. "It was just an observation."

"But it's near ten minutes past. They have never been more than two minutes late."

Isabella lifted her head back over the fence line and scanned once more this time to the south. The path outside their habitat was empty. The office windows, normally alight, were cold and black. "Look at that. I've never seen the lights off."

Sharif spun in a quick, enthusiastic circle, waving his mane through the air. "I told you, it's true. The humans are gone. This is the day."

Quick to believe any good news, the giraffes fell into a tizzy. They ran around each other bounding and leaping. "The humans are gone! The humans are gone!"

Isabella tilted her neck toward the neighboring aviary. "Eagle, have you heard? The humans are missing."

A bald eagle of notable size, beyond prime and weakened by her confines but majestic nonetheless, glided down from her nest in the adjacent aviary. She ruffled her brown feathers and cleared her dormant vocal cords. "I noticed. They have disappeared. I haven't the foggiest idea what has happened."

Isabella stomped her hooves and threw her head back. "The zoo must know. This might be the day after all." Sharif and the other giraffes romped behind her, swinging their long necks and whinnying excitement.

"Isabella, you know better than to hope."

"But, Eagle, the humans have never been this late."

"It's a coincidence. This will be a false alarm like every other."

"No. This time is different. Look around you; the office is dark. It has never been like this."

Eagle fluttered up along the net to a higher branch. She looked at the solid gray stone building with smokeless chimneys and lightless rooms. "It does look like no one is inside."

"They're gone," shouted Sharif behind Isabella. "The humans are gone forever." The giraffes galloped behind him across the habitat to tell others the promising news.

"But why would they leave?" asked Eagle, staring down her golden beak at the giraffe.

"I haven't any idea," said Isabella, her patience waning. "What does it matter? The animals have waited centuries. This is the greatest hope we have had. This could be the day. Tell the pigeons to spread the news."

"Very well." Eagle flew high into the aviary and screeched straight into the air, "Pigeon!"

Tiny gray birds of countless number free from metal fences and twine nets unlike the other animals, flew off the branches of a nearby poplar grove. As the only free creatures in the zoo, the pigeons were relied upon for all communications. It was quite a feat to maintain message delivery in that large of a place, but innate duty filled their veins, and they acted more as one unit than individual birds. Together in a swarm they flew over the zoo habitats toward Eagle. As the flock soared overhead, monkeys clung to the highest boughs in their jungle forest, furry hands on furrowed brows; otters floated on their backs, pointing to the sky; antelopes ran across their plains of tall, golden grass, keeping pace with the birds, all of them wondering the cause of the commotion.

In two minutes they landed on the aviary net. "Yes, ma'am," said the lead pigeon, its eyelids blinking over wide green eyes. "What message do you wish delivered?"

Eagle clicked her golden beak. "Send all your pigeons. Inform the animals the humans are missing."

"Yes, ma'am, right away, ma'am." The flock dispersed on the soft but strengthening breeze.

Like bacteria, the gray drove spread the news, catching the attention of creatures large and small, desperate for the newest buzz to spark life into their morning. Chatter multiplied in a crescendo until an uproarious, opinioned babble hummed through the zoo, pressing beaks, claws and snouts against fences.

"No humans, none at all."

"That's what I hear."

"This could be it."

"Oh, don't raise your hopes on coincidence."

"This must be it. This is the first time the humans have gone missing."

"They can't go missing."

"They will come out of the office soon enough."

"But if they do not…"

"It will be like the other times. You wait and see."

"But if it is not…"

Much time had passed since the animals first entered Clarendon Zoo, which was, of course, the zoo's official name. Many generations had lived and died, and none of the animals knew where they came from or how they came to live inside the zookeeper's circular creation. The animal's entire world lay within those tall outer walls. Some animals guessed great lands and adventure existed outside. Others, the vast majority, were confident nothing existed outside the zoo; that past the walls existed black, open space, a great expanse of nothingness.

Whatever the answer, most never thought of such things;

the animals were far more concerned about their present existence. By and large, they were content. Food came on scheduled
increments. Bedding and other comforts were provided at birth.
When one fell ill, care was promptly given. It was a prosperous
zoo. The animals were seldom in need.

There were, however, many complaints amongst the populace. Animals found it difficult to ignore the fences and bolted
doors, and the reviled chains and cages. They believed they deserved freedom and autonomy, not first-breath subjugation.
Above any complaint, however, the animals felt they deserved
more. Good was the enemy of great, as they often said. The
zookeeper had given them good but limited them from grand
achievements. They believed they could rule better than the
zookeeper. They dreamed visions of liberty and believed together they could create a land more marvelous than the zoo.
The leaders had staged numerous vain rebellions throughout the
years, so many that most had become distant folklore. Many animals had lost the spirit to fight for something greater; but there
were inklings of hope, whispers that an opportunity for self-rule
would one day arise. They had done this for many seasons,
watching spring turn to summer, then into fall, then the cold nip
of winter, each day on the prowl for that single opportunity.
Many hopes had come, and all had disappointed, but this morning was unlike other mornings.

Opinions whirred. Eyes scoured the skies for any bead of
news. Animals clung to the slightest thread of promise. No one
knew what would come, and only the animal with discretionary
power over the zoo could make any forthcoming decision. As
the pigeons sped overhead dispersing speculation, the animals

waited, eager for the news to reach Maximus the grizzly's bear cave.

Meanwhile, Tweed, a portly black and white panda bear, apt to reading and writing, finely honed with the weapon of smooth tongue, watched the commotion from his solitary habitat. He had a nose for opportunity, an ear for self-advantage, and a keen eye to detect both. No day he had seen in his entire lifetime had ever looked so promising.

Twenty seasons of annals lay at his feet, as his teeth chattered on a stalk of chewed bamboo. His paws flipped page over page, fervent, quicker, anxious for the desired information. He reached the end and flung the annals shut. "Five minutes! The latest they have ever been is five minutes!" He fell into neck-twisting contemplation: It's near quarter day and the humans, even the minor ones, are missing. The potentials this could hold…Gracious, this might actually be the day…He stared through his barred door to the east, to the large hill in the center of the zoo and the wide cave at its peak. "Maximus must be contacted, I can't imagine a more clear opportunity." At the thought's conclusion, certain to strain and pester his conscience until provided an answer, Tweed yelled into the air in no particular direction knowing one of them would come. "Pigeon!"

By the time Tweed's message arrived at the hill a few minutes later, Maximus, the great grizzly, had been made well aware of the zoo's present state, nullifying the first half of the repetitive communication.

"Maximus, sir," said Tweed's pigeon out of breath. "There are—"

"No humans in the zoo," finished the grizzly.

"Yes, sir." The pigeon continued. "Tweed wonders if you need his counsel in the matter?"

The stoic grizzly patted down his thick brown fur and stood to four paws. Taut muscles flexed beneath his thick coat. Leathered paws gave the appearance that he had spent his seasons hard at work against captivity's stupor. Firm eyes, both compassionate and menacing, made him an animal feared yet revered. Over the decades, his fairness, honesty, and integrity had built a reservoir of respect. His character had won the animals' admiration, and nothing, neither death, nor torture, nor bribery, could cause him to sacrifice that reputation. He was incorruptible, the type of animal that followed unconditional principles, black and white rules he had given himself to govern the zoo and life. The principles were sacred to him. He preferred gruesome death to violating a single one. Most of the principles he kept hidden, engraved on the slate of his conscience, preferring action to fickle words. But it was widely known he believed, "actions should reflect the animal's desires, regardless of personal opinion." It was his foremost principle. Every decision adhered to it, and any decision involving the zoo's fate would certainly adhere to it.

He looked out of his cave to the land below. The unprecedented event had the whole zoo in a fit of madness. Dozens of pigeons waited expectantly in queue at the cave mouth, bobbing necks and primping wings, with more messages in need of response. The wolf pack, about thirty wolves in total, lined the fence on the hill's western side, sniffing for signs. To the east, one hundred sheep frantically bustled through their pasture with the most recent news and opinions spurting off tongues. "This is it," shouted one. "Ready yourselves. This is the day the zoo is freed!"

Maximus released a hearty laugh that sprang down the limestone hill. "I wondered where important events had run to. I had begun to rot in this cave." His roving eyes returned to the pigeon. "Tell Tweed his counsel is unnecessary at present." He looked to the pigeon queue, already grown by five. "The rest of you, forgive me, I lack the daylight for your messages. We need Chimp's services to solve this mystery. Delay your present deliveries. Make haste to the habitat leaders. If they are in agreement, which I believe they will be, I will summon Chimp. If any animal can explain the current events, it is he."

The obedient pigeons ascended at once, in compact cluster, headed to the distant edges of the zoo.

Maximus stepped further out of the cave onto a short ledge that jutted over the land. His hill, "the hill," as the animals called it, rose up the zoo's middle like an ant dome. The grizzly leader had, upon his appointment, insisted he take a smaller cave with a lesser view, but per tradition the animal's leader lived in the cave atop the hill. From there he saw far into the zoo. Over twenty-five species lived in the separate habitats: koalas, capybaras, peacocks, flamingos, armadillos, ostriches and many more, about one thousand animals in all. Sheep Pasture lay east of the hill. Wolves and their pine forest were immediately to the west. Past them in every direction, other habitats, sequestered by fences, spread through the land. Lush pastures burgeoned daisies and buttercups. Fertile fields of grass swayed in the heavy breeze. Blue lakes reflected fluffy clouds, and soft ripples coursed smoothly and symmetrically across the surfaces. It was a beautiful land, Maximus thought, full of life, full of potential. He was proud to call it home and felt immense conviction to protect it and guide it well.

He stepped further onto the ledge and scanned to the south. The office lay directly opposite the hill across the road. As far as Maximus could tell, humans in uniform were absent from the building. He saw only the opaque windows shielded by wrought-iron bars and the single white door, bright as fresh snow on the office façade. But why today, he thought, of all the times and seasons? Why are they gone so suddenly now?

He was a cautious animal, neither hesitant nor afraid; still he liked to make sense of every angle before reaching a conclusion. For years, every human delay, unusual office signal—any anomaly an animal could conjure—had become glints of hope and in the end false alarms. He knew better than to fall for whims. Nonetheless, he had hope. He had thought freedom would require a battle, a forceful revolution against the humans, where beast drove enslaver scurrying for the outer walls. Many years of preparation had readied him for such an encounter, but from what he saw today, it appeared the humans had evaporated, without warning, sign, or reason.

Word returned faster than even Maximus anticipated his venerable reputation to prompt. A pigeon flock landed on the hillside around noon. "Look at that," Maximus said with a chortle, "might be the fastest delivery I've seen. You must have had your best pigeons on this."

"Always, sir," the lead pigeon replied.

"Are the others in agreement?"

"Yes. They think Chimp is the best option. They said if no

human had been seen by the time we got to the hill, Chimp should be contacted."

"On your flight here you saw no sign of humans?"

"No sign, that's correct."

"I agree; I have seen no sign of those smooth-skinned creatures. Please, find Chimp. I presume he is in or near the office. Ask him to come to me. He tends to listen better in my presence."

"Yes, sir." The birds took to the sky to find the curious creature named Chimp.

The zookeeper, leader of the zoo's affairs, managed matters from inside the office. He kept to the office. The animals thought he appreciated solitude, or disliked attention. In fact, the animals had never seen the zookeeper leave the office, nor had they ever seen him in any capacity. Instead, all office interactions went through Chimp while the zookeeper remained an arcane orchestrator. It seemed the zookeeper felt a peculiar bond with the ape, perhaps because he was the animal nearest human appearance, perhaps because of his superior intellect, or perhaps because of his propensity to loyalty. Whatever the reason, the ape lived inside the office in a reserved room and, as long as he behaved, was permitted abnormal freedom to roam the zoo. As no other animal could speak human, everyone relied upon Chimp as the main conduit to interpret and relay office communications. This ability to decipher the zookeeper's messages had gained him great influence. He was a common attendant in Maximus's cave when complicated matters arose. It had been over a year since Maximus requested Chimp's services, but the day's events demanded every resource.

On this day the inside of the office was cluttered and looked like humans had abandoned it not that morning, as rumors claimed, but days before. Schedule sheets and health records were scattered across tables. Reeking garbage cans sat in the break room corners. A steady pipe drip penetrated through the foam ceiling tile and inched its puddle across the cracked linoleum. The master key ring lay on the break room table, apparently forgotten by the lackadaisical handlers.

When Maximus's pigeon landed on the office windowsill, Chimp was leaning back in a wicker chair, dripping oil droplets onto the rusted key ring. His face was chiseled and his jaw tight. He walked on two hind legs like a man as often as possible, as though to remind lay animals of his elevated status and unique entitlements. In speech, however, he was humble and quiet and was kind and generous by all appearances. He spent much of his time on the road amongst the animals. But in recent months he had kept to the office, rarely leaving or speaking.

The pigeon hammered its beak on the window. "Chimp, Maximus wants to talk to you."

Chimp peeked around a stack of vaccination records. The pigeon messenger latched to the windowsill peered through the milky pane. "Are you there, Chimp? Maximus said come as fast as you can."

The short ape tested the ring. The keys slid well on the oiled surface; he would have quick access to whichever door he wished. He stood, slid in his chair, and cracked open the office's white door. The startled pigeon fell off the sill and flapped to avoid the ground. Chimp opened the door just enough to peek out one eye and peered both ways down the road. "Tell Maximus I will be there shortly."

"Right away, sir." The bird flew toward the hill. Chimp slid his body through the cracked door, shut it behind him, locked the bolt, quickly glanced both ways again, tested the knob, looked a third time, and waited. He stood there five minutes before he was satisfied. Then he stepped down the stairs and started toward Maximus's cave.

Envious eyes watched him stroll down the road, softly clinking keys of freedom hanging from his flexed fingertips. A chorus of murmurs wriggled through the bars.

"Chimp, what's happening?"

"Where are they?"

"Are the humans gone forever?"

"Bring those keys over here."

"Open our door. Set us free."

Intent on the task, Chimp ignored the questions and pleas, leaving the animals to add the ingredient of his silence to the boiling pot of rumors.

It was a quick walk to the hill. Chimp made his way through the locked door, through the field, up the hill, and to the cave mouth, where Maximus greeted him with a heavy pat on his back. "There he is. Thank you for coming so fast."

Chimp bowed at the waist with his hands clasped before him. "Anything for Maximus the grizzly."

"I know you're knowledgeable of the situation. I'll save my breath in explanation. I need to know: have you learned anything? Can you confirm the office is empty?"

"I know almost as little as you. There is, however, one fact that may intrigue you." Chimp hesitated. He looked at Maximus's strong jaw and the white canines that peeked out beneath his lip. He glanced back over his shoulder toward the office, deliberating consequence and reward and possible outcomes. Then the words suddenly poured out of his mouth, "The zookeeper is in his office."

"Impossible. No one has seen or smelt a human since sun broke over the fence."

"I tell you what I know. The humans are gone. But the office is not empty; the zookeeper is here."

Maximus took to brief reflection like he found the final piece of a puzzle and struggled to make it fit no matter how he turned or forced it. "Why would the zookeeper remain while the scent of other humans has disappeared from the zoo?"

Chimp's eyes darted. He shuffled the keys in his hairy hands. "I have no answer for you except my own observation of the zookeeper."

"Where did you observe him? In the office?"

"He has a way of invisibility unless he desires to reveal himself. But the door left open, the pungent smell of that brown liquid machine, the one with the continuous drip, and the occasional soft unnatural thud common to human feet, point to his meandering through his office."

"Then you must contact the zookeeper."

"Maximus, I mean no disrespect in this, but I fear you misjudge the degree of difficulty. The office is large inside, larger than it appears, with many rooms and passages. He is hard to find. Sometimes he's in the room on the left, sometimes the third level, and sometimes I can't find him anywhere in the office at all. If I do somehow find him, he's difficult to engage. Should I somehow manage to engage him, he's difficult to comprehend."

"I understand, Chimp. Nonetheless, of all the events in my time as leader, I venture to say in the history of the zoo, nothing compares in importance to the matter we face on this momentous day. Freedom is within our grasp. We must understand the human's departure. Will they be here by sundown? Tomorrow? Will they return in a season? Or are the humans gone forever? The zookeeper can tell us these things. He must be contacted."

"I understand. I will do my best." Chimp clutched the keys and hustled away.

Time dragged into the afternoon, and humans remained absent. Neither bird nor land animal reported a sighting. Each passing minute seemed to bring greater promise and greater tension. Nervous dissension started to rise as reports turned into tales and threatened to morph into tall tales if limbo lasted any longer. The animals remained without concrete information well into the afternoon.

Two hours before dusk, Chimp ambled back to the hill. The infamous jingle of the keys tortured the animals once more as their snouts grew numb pressed against the bars. Wolves and sheep crowded along the hill's fence so that a large audience formed around the ape as Maximus met him halfway down the slope.

Chimp began before Maximus with a timorous voice, and bystanders wondered why his knees trembled and his palms appeared to sweat. "I located the zookeeper from a distance."

"What do you mean from a distance?" asked Maximus.

"As I have told you before, he's a difficult man to find, let alone speak with."

"Were you able to speak to him? What did he say?"

"It was brief, but the best I could do, and you must understand," Chimp opened his hands in a wide circle to address the audience around him, "my human language has been somewhat deficient as of recent. I'm unsure why, but it has been less than optimal."

"But you understood him?" interrupted the sheep leader named Tully. She stood along the eastern fence, pressing her crisp white wool against the chain links. She had a cute pink nose and long ears that stuck out to the sides. There was initial adorableness in her looks and peace in her stride, but she had iron zeal in her eyes, harshness, almost a fire, that made it difficult to look at her for long.

"Bits and pieces, yes…" He paused. He glanced at the sheep and wolves and the grizzly towering over him. "It seems the humans are gone. They will not return. The zoo will remain open, and the zookeeper alone will provide our needs. I struggled to make out what he meant at the end, the language grew fuzzy and distance greater as he walked to another room, but I suspect he meant there will be nothing more and nothing less."

"Wonderful!" shouted a mid-seasoned wolf cub through the western fence. The wolves began to wrestle and howl.

"Wait, wait one moment." Maximus rose and waved his paw to quiet the onlookers. "Forgive me, I have two immediate questions. Why did the humans leave? And why has the zookeeper suddenly decided to free us?"

"Maximus, these are complicated matters. I can only repeat myself so much," insisted Chimp. "The zookeeper is a quiet, reclusive man, never has he elaborated. But neither has he provided a reason to doubt his word."

"I do not doubt his word. It's his intentions I question."

The wolf leader, Ironpaw, who maintained a healthy but tensioned rivalry with Maximus, pushed his snout through the fence and interjected. "Why do you question him?" The wolf had orange eyes and a scarred snout that had a story. His coat was chestnut brown other than his strong right paw which was metallic silver. He was a head shorter, a bit weaker, a tad less courageous, a pinch less respected, and, because of his overall inferiority to Maximus, copiously more Napoleonic. "We have waited our entire lives to have freedom. Do you want our captivity to continue?"

Grumbles roused amongst the animals. Maximus faced the brown wolf. "Easy there, Ironpaw. No one wants to see an emotional animal do something reckless. I fully support animal freedom."

"Explain then your lack of desire."

"Yes, explain yourself," demanded Tully, coldly glaring at the grizzly.

Maximus looked between the two leaders. "I wonder why the zookeeper remains."

"What does it matter?" snapped Ironpaw. He turned to Chimp. "Has the man at last decided to let us rule ourselves?"

Chimp had inched his way out of Maximus's reach. "Yes. It appears that's exactly what has happened."

"There you have it, straight from the mouth of the office,

the zookeeper has finally gained a bit of sense and given us freedom to rule ourselves. So what does it matter why? We are free."

Maximus watched Chimp's fingers slide the keys in a slow circle, one after another, round, and round, and round. He looked at the expectant faces lit with excitement. He had never envisioned it happening this way. He thought it peculiar that the zookeeper should simply grant them uninhibited freedom without apparent motivation or price on a normal day, at a normal hour, from all angles on a complete whim. But it was just a perturbed prodding in his gut, something instinctual he could not put to words, something he could not prove, something he knew others would fail to understand. He thought about it a second longer, and at last, suffocated by the weight of popular opinion, he spoke. "Where are the pigeons?"

"That's more like it," said Ironpaw, a twinkle in his eye, gloating over his small victory. Maximus stepped toward him and growled. The inferior animal backed down dragging his nose in the dirt.

A flood of pigeons, what seemed like all available flocks, circled above, separate from the conversation but hearing every word. The head pigeon dropped onto the hillside. "Should we spread the news?"

"Yes, as fast as possible," responded Maximus. "Tell the animals we have been freed. From this day forward the zoo is ours."

Elated howls burst from the wolves. The sheep bayed and danced through the pasture. "Chimp, unlock the habitats," declared Maximus. "Then make ready..." He prepared to give other instructions, but the animals yelled and shook the fences.

"Unlock our door!"

"Us first!"

"Over here. Free us!"

Chimp fumbled the keys and rushed over to free the animals. One key entered a lock, then the next, then the next. Cage doors opened. Animals spilled onto the road like streams into a dried gorge. Lying on the warm pavement, they kissed the dirty asphalt again and again, reaching hooves and paws to the sky, as if to cradle liberation.

Chimp worked diligently. Soon, freed animals joined the cause, unable to watch a fellow animal caged for a moment longer. Isabella scooped Chimp on her back and ran him around the zoo. Ironpaw tore the worn aviary net in a swift, violent motion, freeing the exotic birds into the endless blue sky they had long been denied. Eagle swooped down, took the proper keys, and flew to the far reaches to unlock the furthest habitats. Intermingling of a dreamy kind began, for only in dreams was it ever possible. Creatures known only by name or tale became known by introduction. The animals celebrated their good fortune with any animal they saw. Monkeys hugged flamingos, antelopes sprinted down the road to greet chameleons, kangaroos were seen kissing the cheeks of sloths and otters alike. The hope of a thousand seasons had come to pass in their lifetime.

By late afternoon, Eagle glided on lethargic wings, Isabella attempted to control her belabored breaths, and Chimp's weary arms hung limp at his sides. All habitats were unlocked. Every animal roamed free.

In his cave Maximus splashed water on his face. A new chapter had arrived in the zoo's history, a momentous one bound to alter their existence. He felt it proper to make a speech, nothing noteworthy but something that would remind the animals what they had left behind and the great challenge and opportunity that lay ahead. Animal autonomy meant order would need to be established, but more than laws or structure a vision had to be cast, a vision animals could strive to fulfill. It needed to be a call to duty and action, mandatory for any who wished to be a part of the great land they were set to create, a vision that would inspire generations to come.

Owl, a shrewd, loud barn owl, keen to capture animals' attention by whatever means possible, offered to gather the animals for the grizzly leader's speech. The large-eyed bird took off into the sky and fluttered his wings to rejuvenate atrophied muscles. The day was waning with the last fleeting hour of light as he made the announcement in a continuous drowned hum over the crowds. "Attention, zoo animals, Maximus the grizzly has a proclamation to make. Assemble at the hill."

Freed zoo inhabitants from the north, south, east, and west made the journey in top speed to the tallest hill in the land. Smaller creatures climbed atop new friends to secure a better view. Two lucky flying squirrels secured the best seat atop Sharif's head. Prairie dogs and baby koalas crawled atop the fluffy backs of sheep, leaving the last of the small creatures seats atop antelopes' backs. Eclectic animals sprawled over the hill's slope, packed tight, spilling out of the habitat onto the road, anxious to hear their leader's words.

As last light melted into the western outer wall, Maximus stepped out of his cave onto the ledge that overlooked the zoo. Behind him the stone hill glimmered in the setting sun, and the faintest light of the full moon materialized in the east. The sea of animals stood. Maximus saw peacock's rainbow feathers beside zebra's striped coats, the flying squirrel's petite bodies atop the giraffe's long frames, the snake's black, rubbery skin aside sheep's crisp white wool. They were united, together as one. The grizzly reared onto his hind legs above his beloved animals. What followed was less a speech, as it was a simple declaration from the mind of a humble leader who could put the complexities of life into simple words.

"My dear animals, I have only a few words to say as the sun sets on this momentous day. We have lived many seasons under the rule of oppressive humans. They stole our liberty, used our labors for personal profit, and made us believe our rightful place was beneath them. Today, that is no more. The old has gone; the new has come.

"Tomorrow you will rise. The sun will glint your eyes as it has every day. But tomorrow you will no longer be zoo animals. You will be citizens, equal citizens of a mighty land, a land ruled by free animals. Cage doors will never be locked. Toils will be for animals' reward alone. Life shall prosper on this soil. Liberty will reign in this place. On this hallowed ground, the citizen who pursues it shall achieve happiness. Seasons will pass but this land, our land, will remain a symbol of freedom and justice, proof that free animals can govern, flourish, and live as one."

As the sun set on open habitats and solidarity, the swath of land was renamed to the passionate hoots, roars, shrieks, wails, growls, bays, barks, hisses and howls of its citizens, Zoon Garden, a land of life, liberty, and happiness for all animals.

2

IN THE MONTHS after the Day of Freedom, Maximus remained skeptical of the zookeeper. He wondered why the man had given them freedom, and why he remained in Zoon, as his vassal Chimp said, but had never been seen. The conundrum chaffed his mind. But in Zoon's first months no one heard a whisper of the man or saw the faintest shadow, and Maximus let the office and its mysteries fall to the back of his mind.

There was a great deal of initial excitement in the early days. Maximus worked harder than anyone to make Zoon, as they had taken to calling it, the greatest land animal feet had ever touched. Hopeful citizens, inspired by their toiling leader, trusted Maximus's vision. They believed in his principles of unity, respect and integrity, and citizens of every species labored hard together to mold the burgeoning land into a paradise for all animal kind.

The citizens proved far smarter than one's typical animals. Many of them were quite brilliant, capable of reading, writing,

and understanding complex ideas. Their ingenuity swiftly transformed the zoo. Roads were created, connecting habitats from
east to west. Canals were dug, supplying fresh drinking and
bathing water to each habitat. The technologically minded monkeys constructed Pigeon Tower, a five-hundred-foot, heavy timber structure near Zoon's center, where pigeons fashioned nests
inside a large house atop the tower and marveled at their new-
found ability to send direct, near instant, messages anywhere in
the land.

Zoon became an interconnected web, whereby citizens
could travel anywhere with ease, or speak to a distant friend
simply by waving a hoof or paw toward Pigeon Tower. The days
stayed filled with hard work. Citizens found joy in the flex of
stiff muscles. They took pride in creations built for themselves
and by themselves and bent the land to their will. Koalas, aided
by sloths, created an oasis where citizens could massage away
discomfort. In Antelope Fields, a track was constructed for the
land's greatest athletes to compete. Giraffes threw weeklong cel-
ebrations full of laughter, music, and every manner of gaiety,
inviting every species to partake during their off hours.

Zoon Garden looked fit to accomplish the feats Babel had
failed. Habitats welcomed citizens from every corner. Resources
were plentiful. Needs were few. Quality of life was better than
it had ever been. Citizens could seldom dream what else an animal might want. The garden had food, water, fulfilling labor,
entertainment, company, cultural pride, equality, and purpose,
but mostly it had hope, a place of limitless opportunity where
any honest animal, not afraid to put hoof to dirt, could shed his
tethers, forget the past, start afresh on equal ground, and forge

the life he wished. The citizens were merry, filled with bright visions of the future.

Then something peculiar occurred. It is yet to have been mentioned: this zoo had many strange happenings; not quite magical, they were normal but nonetheless odd, indeed, quite odd, and came without rhyme or reason as if they floated out of the air. But once they arrived, they stayed and became as real as the sun, trees, and animals. On a warm day at the beginning of fall, the Plague of Realization descended upon Zoon and began to infect the citizens' psyches. It was certainly a funny named disease but had less comical consequences.

When the imperceptible plague arrived, the cheetah leader, a cat named Raka, was passing by Sloth Jungle. Deep black circles surrounded the spotted feline's eyes, and his long tail twitched with impatience. He was an honorable leader but turbulent when stirred and had exceptional stubbornness that had dug him into more than one disagreement. Fifty feet from the overgrown jungle a rancid, festering reek struck his nostrils. His snout scrunched, and tears came to his amber eyes. "What is that awful smell?" Insulted by the odor, he choked down his revulsion and walked inside to have a word with whichever citizen had let such a horrid stench develop in their home.

At once, Raka was revolted by the place. Fungus grew like boils on the trees, and slimy algae grew thick and brown in the water pools. He quickly plugged his nose, a frantic and, as he soon realized, fruitless attempt to curb the fetid scent. He hopped on three paws for thirty seconds down what he gauged must be the path. The trail, of sorts, opened into a small clearing. Ahead in the trees, Raka saw ten sloths hanging by long claws on the branches. Green moss and fungi grew on their fur, and they stayed so still the branches appeared to sway faster. Had he not seen the whites of their eyes he would have thought them part of the overgrowth. In his next breath he realized the stench of decay, the palpable revulsion, was not the forest but these sedentary citizens.

Raka thought their silence discourteous so he spoke. "Good morning. I was on the road and thought I would pay you a visit."

The sloths' eyes moved; at least Raka thought they moved. In five seconds their heads turned…In five more they smiled beneath squinted eyes…And in ten more their mouths opened. "Ggggggooooooooooooooodddddd…"

Oh no, thought Raka, oh my, no. Impatience boiled out of the cheetah's veins. The stench was horrendous, the malaise toxic, the environment revolting. He had seen enough. Think. Think of an excuse, any excuse, something to leave, it doesn't have to be good.

"…mmmmmmmmoooooooorrrrrrr…"

Any excuse, you fool, think of something, anything. Their smiles were wide, squinting their eyes, and their hands moved nanometers per second. "…nnnnnnnnniiiiiiiiiiiinnnnnnnnn…"

Raka shot his head around looking at the trees, paths, jungle. How in the world do I escape this place? Heavens, there's no time for cordiality, he thought. I must go, go now. "Ok, thank you," he sputtered. "I must be going. I forgot I had a…uh…an important…very important…I must be off." He backed away one cautious step at a time, realized they were incapable of yelling a rebuke anyhow, turned, and sprinted down the road without a single backward glance.

He burst into Cheetah Habitat out of breath, "Jonesy, brother, where are you?" Flustered and disoriented, Raka ran through the tall grass, looking every which way until he found his elder brother, a seasoned cheetah with taut cheeks and patchy fur, in the shade of an umbrella tree.

"What in heavens happened to you?" asked Jonesy, leaping up from the tree's trunk.

Raka paced, snorting every few seconds to exhale the lingering smell. "The sloths, Jonesy. It was the sloths. Have you been to their jungle? Right there on the corner, beside the chameleons. Have you seen how they live?"

Jonesy peered down the road toward the sloths' habitat. "Never have. What about them?"

"Slow, everything they do is slow."

"Eh? What's wrong with that? I'm sure these old bones have made me a bit slower."

"No, Jonesy, it's worse than you could ever imagine. It made my fur curl to be in that place, and to be near them, those slow smiles…the words…It took them half an hour to get out 'good morning'."

"Sounds horrid."

"It was! I haven't a clue about their names or what they do throughout the day but hang in those trees and rot; I mean it, Jonesy, by the smell of it I think their flesh was rotting. Citizens should know better than to act so disrespectfully slow. Imagine if those…" he waved his paw in a circle signifying the atrocity unworthy of words, "…those things influenced other citizens. Imagine if we had a whole land full of lazy sloths."

"It would be terrible."

"It would be our death sentence. The land would be a dump in a week. I can tell you this much, Jonesy, if you want to stay happy, keep away from sloths."

That same day, five hours later, further east, Ironpaw stood on the road sweeping excess dust with a pine branch gripped between his jaws. Like his disciplined wolf brethren, he was an achiever, always on the search for tasks, ways to improve, advantages to pursue. He thought Zoon looked proper with tidy roads and had assigned himself the duty of enforcing their cleanliness. Having finished the part in front of Wolf Habitat, he noticed a large accumulation of half-chewed leaf stems in front of Koala Habitat. In the trees above, ten koalas lay dead asleep snoring the day away.

Mid-afternoon, plenty of sunlight, and they're asleep, Ironpaw thought. There is work to be done. How is this land to function with citizens sleeping in the middle of the day? He took a few steps forward and barked across the road, gruff and brash. "You in the tree, wake up. Your road needs cleaning."

The startled gray, chubby-cheeked fur balls rolled over yawning and scratching their hinds. The fattest one opened his tired eyes and smacked his lips. "Wha—what did you say?"

"I said wake up. This is no time to be sleeping. You slept twelve hours last night. Get out of bed and clean your portion of the road."

The half awake koala cast his kin a bewildered glance. "Afternoon is our nap time. The road looks fine. It's just a few stems."

"It is dirty and disorganized."

"Oh well, sorry." The koalas nuzzled against the tree and

resumed their naps.

Ironpaw ground his teeth. You stupid, fat, bums, he thought, and stormed down the road.

The two occurrences, mere observations really, were seen as nothing more than irksome interactions. Both individuals did their utmost to push the unfortunate events from their consciences. Ironpaw ignored the lazy koalas. Raka turned the opposite direction whenever he saw a sloth. But then the realizations continued.

The next day new interactions of varying severity sprang up throughout the land. They seemed rather trivial, but to the witnesses they were no laughing matter.

Isabella had spent extensive time training in Antelope Fields and with the help of her long strides had emerged as one of the better athletes in the land. Talented youths trained with her on a regular basis, hoping their skill would reach fruition with her guidance. The antelopes had proven capable in middle distance events, and many of her best pupils were those short-tailed, long-horned bovids. Isabella thought them talented, but they had developed a habit that infuriated her: they walked with their heads down, horns pointed straight out, accidently poking other citizens.

This particular morning she watched three of the antelopes pass by and leaned over to her mate. "Sharif, that one. Yes, the one right there on the end, he's the one I told you about. He stabbed me four times. The one in the middle has speared me six." She bent her neck around and pointed with her nose to an array of gashes along her hindquarters. "Here. There. Right here. This one is an inch deep."

"Does it hurt?" asked Sharif.

"You best believe it. Hurts when it happens and hurts for weeks after."

"Do they apologize?"

"Of course they apologize; they're not monsters. But look at them." She whipped her head back round. "They continue to do it, noses down, horns forward. Look, the one on the right is about to hit that post." The antelope, oblivious to where it walked, trudged right into a wooden pole. The trapped citizen shoved his hoof on the pole, jerked and kicked, then heaved, and with the help of its two friends dislodged. "You see!" cried Isabella. "Clueless! And look how deep it went. That post was my leg last week. That was my leg! And I'm not the only one either. Zebras, cheetahs, wolves—anyone who comes to compete has been stabbed by those horns. I swear the antelopes are blind to where they walk, but they're not blind; they can see perfectly well. They're careless and stupid. The first time, ok, but four times—six! And who knows how many times they've stabbed other citizens. Why must we suffer because the antelopes cannot control their spiked heads?"

Sharif exhaled. "It's inconsiderate."

"Absolutely. To think, a species could be so inconsiderate they walk about stabbing other citizens. Incredible!"

Three hours later, a heated argument arose in Zebra Habitat over the prairie dogs' delusional idea of homemaking. "I counted them, twenty-seven. There are twenty-seven holes throughout the grassland," said a tall zebra, nose pointed toward his ankle. "I was running at my normal pace, about to open for a sprint, when my hoof slipped into one of their tunnels. I nearly shattered my leg."

"Unbelievable," said an older zebra. "They come as guests and dig holes across our lands."

"Not in one spot either, throughout the fields. I nearly twist an ankle everywhere I walk."

"Why do they need more holes anyway? They have plenty in their habitat. Go fill them. Let us hope the message sinks through their tiny skulls."

Ten minutes later in the eastern pastures, Tully stood atop her knoll watching her white fluffs, the plentiful sheep populace, graze in the grass. She spent most her time amongst the sheep, tending to their needs, guiding them like a shepherd. A posse of advisors, led by another sheep named Snowy, frolicked after her wherever she went. They had cheery faces and strong hearts but very seldom advised. Snowy submitted to Tully, and the advisors followed form, bleating in agreement to whatever Tully said.

She had begun to address them when a wolf walked into the pasture toward the flock. Tully's tail perked up, and she tapped her lead advisor. "Snowy, Snowy, look at this," she said, a hint of angst in her voice. "What is that wolf doing?"

"I don't know, ma'am. Look at those fangs and those claws. I get a cold chill in my spine whenever I see one of those wolves. They look violent, Tully."

"I feel it too. They look dangerous, and mean too."

"Do you think they would, you know, attack?"

"No, no, that's far beyond the wickedness of a Zoon citizen. But there is something off about them. They're arrogant, aggressive"—Tully suddenly pointed her hoof at the wolf—"have blatant disregard for others; look at him." The wolf, jogging through the middle of the flock, was, ignorantly or purposefully (it was difficult to tell which) bumping into sheep, bowling over the weakest ones. "Do...do you see this?" Tully stammered, nearly running down the hill. "That wolf is abusing smaller citizens."

The fickle realizations were popping up everywhere. Everyone was noticing or imagining small, unanticipated annoyances, little irritations they could not ignore. But it was not the fault of a few select species. Everyone was having realizations about everyone. Prairie dogs were furious when zebras backfilled their elaborate tunnel system. Sloths thought the impatient cheetahs too stubborn to learn life's gradual lessons. The koalas thought the wolves too ambitious and in need of relaxation before they worked life away.

After days noticing the same irritations about the same citizens, they confirmed these were not mere observations or even unfortunate interactions; they were confirmed revelations of reality. The sloths truly were dreadfully slow and quite literally enjoyed living amongst scum. Cheetahs were impatient and easily aggravated, refusing to listen to anyone. Giraffes were judgmental, fickle, and superficial, focused more on a good time than important matters. Antelopes teetered on the lower intelligence spectrum and rarely put a thought toward their surroundings. Selfish and relentless, the wolves had high standards, a strong superiority complex, and an inclination to scorn inferiors. Sheep were labeled emotionally softer than their wool, incessant complainers, and appeared passive but were subliminally quite fierce, especially when prodded.

The realizations shocked everyone. When the zoo had been freed, citizens anticipated different cultures and diverse interests, but no one had expected such substantial differences. For the time the land remained harmonious. But as citizens continued their daily lives, the virus, the Plague of Realization, took imperceptible effect. Citizens had irritable, fur-curling realizations about their fellow citizens, and they wondered how long they would be able to live alongside neighbors of such annoying tendencies.

3

A WEEK AFTER the Plague of Realization descended on Zoon, Maximus lumbered down his hill onto the road and immediately noticed something quite odd. Fewer citizens were on the road, far fewer than usual, no antelopes and zebras prancing down the asphalt together, no monkeys and buffalos discussing the day's events. In fact, no species were talking to one another. He saw only small cliques: four kangaroos hopping, six snakes slithering, and five peacocks strutting, all refusing to acknowledge one another.

He opened his mouth to speak to them, but before he could shout, a jittery voice clattered behind him. "Excuse me, Maximus, excuse me, do you have a minute?" Tweed shuffled his girth out of his habitat onto the road. He had gained twenty pounds, and his stomach jostled like a swing as his stubby legs heaved him to his destination. He was out of breath and panted as he waved down the grizzly. "I must speak with you…one minute please…only one."

Maximus scrunched his eyes and turned around. He had

never considered Tweed a friend. The relationship felt closer to a business associate, one he could speak to about formal matters. He often developed a troubled feeling around the spotted bear, the same he felt around Chimp, the same he felt when the zookeeper freed the zoo. Lack of authenticity, too kind in a fictitious way, an altruistic façade—Maximus could not pinpoint what it was that bothered him about Tweed, but the perplexed hunch was undeniable.

"Good morning, Tweed, I have time, more than a minute if you need."

The panda bear stepped closer. His face was round like a dinner plate and his eyes had a slight squint, accentuated by his puffy cheeks. A black patch surrounded one eye, and the rest of the face was white to the top of the head where both colors mixed evenly over his body. He was a steady and perseverant citizen, prone to ideas and schemes, and liable to enamor those whose help he needed with words they wished to hear.

"Thank you, sir. As I said, I don't wish to hold you long; I know you keep a busy schedule. This morning it struck me that Zoon moves fast and many events occur, too many for one citizen to manage. As you know, I listen to the citizen's needs and have good relationships with the leaders. Please know I am here if you ever need assistance. We bears must stick together."

Maximus pointed his claw down the road. "Do you know why the citizens are acting peculiar?"

"Peculiar? In what way?"

"Look at them. They're uneasy. The snakes avoid the kangaroos, kangaroos avoid the snakes…and the peacocks want nothing to do with either of them. Has something happened? Only a week ago they were working together on the road near Buffalo Habitat."

Tweed watched the secluded citizens, neither speaking, nor making eye contact. "That is strange."

"Very strange."

"I have heard nothing. Likely a coincidence, doubtful it's something to let consume your mind."

"Perhaps, but very bizarre nonetheless." Maximus watched them for another second. "I must go, Tweed. You know any citizen is welcome in my cave. Come by whenever you wish." Maximus darted away and galloped down the road to discover why his citizens had contracted, as best he could describe, sudden introverted temperaments.

Tweed peeked after him. When the grizzly had escaped earshot, he turned his head the other way. "Pigeon!" He withdrew a fresh bamboo stalk from a leather satchel secured squarely around his neck and began to chew.

In Tweed's mind, Zoon Garden was a fine establishment, but it could improve; liberty was only the first step. He had a firm vision of the direction Zoon should be steered, a firm idea of how citizens should behave, a firm belief of what should be condoned and what should be condemned, a firm image of what the garden should become. He was confident in this vision and believed if he gained the proper ear, and appeased the right citizens, he could create the perfect land. And he was willing to go to whatever end to see his utopia manifest.

After a minute, Tweed looked to the sky. "Where are these birds?" He shielded the sun with his paw and looked toward the distant tower. "Pigeon!"

A gray bird catapulted out of the air. It dove and spun through the air. "Apologies, sir, I'm coming." It flitted through the sky onto the ground beside Tweed. "Forgive our delay. No one heard your yell."

"Don't make excuses for your tardiness. Find Owl. He's probably far off where I can't reach him. Have him come to me. Make it quick."

"Right away." Prompted by the need to maintain reputation, the pigeon sped to Owl. It was a short flight, for Owl spent most of his time in Pigeon Tower amongst the other birds. Pigeons fluttered in and out of the tower's holes, testing wings and practicing message deliveries. Tweed's pigeon landed on a roost on the tower's western face beside the bird. "Tweed has beckoned you. It sounded urgent." Owl cast the smaller bird a contemptuous glance and darted toward the road.

Citizens had long wondered what problem occurred at the time of Owl's birth. It was a conundrum how a citizen with eyes so large and a mouth so small did so little seeing and so much speaking. He was a smart bird, but unlike his ancestors, he was rash and sometimes imprudent, and no one had ever called him wise. He loved to be heard, no matter the topic or opinion, and was loyal to those who gave him opportunities to promulgate his voice. Since the Day of Freedom, he had had few opportunities to make announcements and had become fidgety with frustration.

In a flush of wing flaps, he landed on the road beside Tweed. Eager for involvement in whatever idea the panda might have, the bird hopped up to him with a glint in his eye. "The pigeon said you called."

Tweed put his paw around the bird. "Yes, I need to tell you something. Here, over here. No telling who's listening. No honest citizen wants an eavesdropper in a private conversation." He shuffled him behind a coniferous tree on the road's edge and wiped dust flecks off his wings. "Much better. How are you?"

"Well, Tweed. The season is warm. My wings have strengthened. To take flight, as I desire, as high or as far as I wish, is wonderful. Meanwhile our land thrives. The citizens are free and well fed. Why yesterday I saw a zebra at her habi—"

"Yes, yes, that's good, glad to hear it." Tweed took another chew of the bamboo shoot. Then he whipped it around and pointed it at the bird's face, so close that Owl moved his beak to the side. "Owl, you have been underutilized in this new land."

"Oh, well, I'm not sure that's entirely true."

"Drop the humility. It's true. I know it and you know it. You have talents that need deployment. A citizen of your capabilities belongs in the center of Zoon's events. Recall when you flew across the garden on the Day of Freedom to unite the citizens for Maximus's declaration? An unprecedented assembly of that nature would have been impossible without your talent to announce vital messages to citizens. I lack concrete evidence, but I feel moments are near when those abilities will again be required. Events will need announcement. Ideas will need proclamation. Citizens must remain updated to avoid ignorance. Zoon needs a bird to inform them of affairs in the garden. I know what you'll say, 'The pigeons do a fine job.' That they do. But their abilities are limited to citizen-to-citizen message delivery; it is their specialty. A different bird, one steadfastly dedicated to Zoon's betterment, must prepare to announce significant events."

"And you think I'm that bird?"

"I know you are that bird. Someone must be aware of activities in Zoon to assure it operates at optimal level. Now, this is what you must do for me. Fly around the garden with sights on citizen's minuscule movements. Look for events of significance, opportunity or notoriety, those that would spark citizenry interest. When you notice a noteworthy event, you must announce it to the land. It's your voice alone that can inform the citizenry."

"You really mean that?"

"I most certainly do. Without you the citizens will be misinformed. They will never know the truth."

"It's an honor, Tweed, a real honor." Owl flapped a foot off the ground in excitement. "When should I begin?"

"Important news is lost as we speak. Fly now before more is lost."

"Yes, right away." Owl took off over the tree in confounded flurry, prepared to discern and communicate every vital event for the sake of his beloved Zoon.

4

THE FALL LEAVES continued to drop, and the wind whipped. The land remained calm, but interesting rumors were starting to spread.

"Do you remember what you told me about koalas?" asked an elder wolf named Halfear. The seasoned wolf was Ironpaw's closest confidant. Oldest in the pack, he was long, thin, and bony with an ashen face, as though he ate his fill and old age struggled to hold it on his bones. He hid ten twisted teeth behind a level scowl, and a scarred tongue tucked behind both. He was alert and guarded in old age; he had seen too many things.

Ironpaw prowled beside him through the center of the pine forest in Wolf Habitat. He stopped at the base of the largest tree in the woods. Its trunk was wide enough for three wolves to stand around snout to tail and rose over two hundred feet. "I told you I caught them sleeping in the afternoon, too tired to clean their road. Lazy tree rats…"

Halfear scratched his rump against the tree. "Yes. And we both agreed it was wise for wolves to stay away from tree rats and other lazy citizens."

"I remember. What happened? Did you catch a wolf with a koala?"

"No, no, never could such a thing happen; the pack is loyal to a fault. It's something else." Halfear glanced behind the tree and lowered his voice to a whisper. "I've kept my ears on alert. The sheep are spreading strange ideas."

Ironpaw's ears perked at the mention of sheep. He could not say why, but whenever he saw one of the fluffy citizens, his lips curled, and he became angry, very angry. The way they walked, talked, looked—everything about them made him furious. "What sort of ideas?"

"Bizarre beliefs...they say every animal is the same, equal in every way: prairie dogs deserve the same food as buffaloes, armadillos deserve as much land as antelopes, flying squirrels deserve as much water as otters."

"What logic is that?"

"It's not logic from what I can tell. Scarily stupid, actually, and they seem adamant about the ideas. They're spreading them through the zoo."

"Have you warned the pack?"

"Not yet. I'll gather them today."

"Good. Tell them no wolf should interact with a sheep. No wolf should talk to or go near one of those fluffy citizens. And if you would, Halfear, keep an eye on their pasture. They give me a bad feeling, no telling what other stupid ideas they might create."

Beneath the harmonious façade, the Plague of Realization, the intoxicating virus, too potent to cure, too rampant to stop, had continued to infect citizens' minds and hearts. Everyone began to realize each species possessed a conglomeration of genetics, experiences, beliefs, cultural dogma, ideology, and personal taste that created a specific vision of how they thought Zoon should be organized and run.

It became apparent that Tully, and thereby, Snowy, the advisors, and the entire sheep flock, believed adamantly in unequivocal, irrevocable equality. They had compassion for all citizens, every one, least to the greatest, especially the least and vowed to protect those who could not protect themselves. They believed Zoon would prosper when all citizens lived completely equal.

Wolves believed in complete autonomy, complete freedom, as they put it. They were big and powerful and had been the top of the hierarchical chain forever. Rooted in the archaic traditions that had served them well for decades, they desired orderliness and consistent social structure. Lazy and weak citizens frustrated them. They lacked patience for the timid or meek and believed the gifted, the pure, the powerful, should rise to the top, and in that way Zoon would prosper.

Superficial giraffes believed life should optimize pleasure and be filled with merry moments. They envisioned a land of endless amusement, filled with forever-happy citizens. Cheetahs were mavericks; it was hard to determine what they would do. The cats hated rules. They loathed oversight. And they detested citizens who supported any limitation over them. Monkeys were creative and ingenious, believing technology and progress were the path to a perfect land. Koalas were relaxed and slow-paced, never worrying, taking life an hour at a time. Beavers were cautious and traditional, always emphasizing routine and order.

Every species from chameleons to buffalos also had visions of how they wished Zoon to function. And somehow, despite the polar opposite conclusions, every species adamantly defended its visions, believing their particular vision was the one path to the perfect land.

Because of the glorious freedom they had received through Maximus, their founding father, every species and individual believed they could achieve their envisioned utopia alongside fellow citizens. But as the plague's contagion infected minds, citizens realized more and more this was far from reality. Species had competing visions. The monkeys could not progress Zoon if the koalas couldn't manage to clean their habitat. Likewise, the koalas couldn't enjoy the present day if the monkeys were forever focused on projects of tomorrow. Sheep could not institute complete equality if the wolves were determined to outshine everyone. Wolves could not achieve unencumbered freedom if sheep were determined to make everyone the same.

As the plague's potency increased, the virus caused the all-encompassing realization: other species hindered the achievement of the perfect land.

Upon this realization citizens began to separate. They spent more time inside their native habitats, comfortable with those who looked like them and thought like them. The transition was hardly perceptible, unintended, and felt almost natural. Barely anyone noticed the estranged species return to their habitats. Maximus, however, noticed every minute detail. He saw the road stay barren for days at a time and rarely saw a citizen visit or speak to a different species. But there was seldom time to dwell on this development. Two days later he awoke to hundreds of squawking pigeons, far more than he ever recalled, covering the sky in small, gray patches like low-hanging cirrus clouds. Below the birds, he saw citizens vigorously waving paws and hooves for messages to be delivered to the neighbors they refused to speak to.

Zoon was a free land; citizens could do what they wished, but Maximus felt an uneasy gurgle in the pit of his gut. Habitats were open, Zoon was liberated, and yet the citizens had encaged themselves back inside their habitats secluded from fellow citizens with whom, despite every annoyance, displeasure or disagreement, they must share the land. Nothing good, Maximus thought, could come of this.

5

A S THE FALL progressed, citizens stayed inside their respective habitats neither seeing, nor hearing, nor speaking to other species. The alienated land remained cordial. But each day thousands of messages transmitted through Pigeon Tower until the great looming spire in the center of the land became Zoon's main communicative form and connected the land like a web. Constant squawks filled the sky, and if one listened closely he or she could sometimes hear other citizens' conversations.

One day Snowy, her pink ears pointed up and thin legs plodding the grass, tramped through the pasture. "That was the meanest thing I have ever heard," she cried in a fit of rage, tears rolling down her cheeks. She kicked a pebble and smacked a puddle. "They shouldn't be allowed to say things like that."

Ten sheep followed close behind intrigued by her muffled tirade. Tully ran up beside her, consoling and attentive to her needs. "We understand your pain. What happened? Who said what?"

"The pigeon," she blubbered. "I heard the pigeon say horrible, nasty things."

Tully nuzzled against her side. "Whose pigeon was it?"

"I don't know whose. It flew over me. It passed the message onto another pigeon. I think it was a wolf; it sounded like something one of those mean wolves would say."

"And what was it they said?"

Snowy pressed into Tully, blotting her tears on her wool. "They said sheep hair looks like wisps of cloud, and the faintest breeze might rip our delicate coats right off."

"That's not true," shouted one of the sheep.

"We have strong wool," shouted another. "It can't be ripped off by wind."

"They can't say that," yelled a third. "That's mean."

Dozens of heads across the pasture stopped munching grass to look up at the tearful hullabaloo. Tully rubbed against her advisor's snout. "This is bad, Snowy, very bad." The sheep leader stood up, trembling with indignation. "What have I told you about verbal abuse?"

Still sniffling, Snowy lifted her chin. "You say, 'Verbal abuse always precedes physical abuse.'"

"That is exactly right. It always starts small—a slight comment, a demeaning word. But if not nipped right away it continues—nastier insults, objectification, prejudice and eventually physical violence." Fifty sheep stood around her and more were gathering. Her shrill voice grew higher with each sentence. "You all must understand it is terrible for strong citizens to oppress weak ones. In the zoo I watched bigger animals receive more food and prettier animals receive more attention. This is wrong and evil. It's an injustice. All citizens are equal; all citizens deserve equal treatment. I dream of a day when every citizen, small or large, old or young, strong or weak, will be equal in every way, same food, same love, same entitlements; all will be fair, all citizens will be the same.

"But let me tell you, hateful verbal abuse like this will kill our dream. Some say these are just silly words, but they are wrong. This is hatred. And hatred is horrendous; hatred is the seed of oppression. Oh, I feared this. The first second I saw those wolves I thought they might try to dominate the land, and now I know for certain." She motioned for the flock to come closer like she had a secret no one else must hear. Her voice quieted, and her eyes flitted between their faces and Wolf Habitat. "This morning I saw two wolves bullying a young koala, yesterday I heard they forced a prairie dog to give her extra food, and the day before someone said he saw a wolf harass a chameleon because of his 'colorful skin.' Don't you see what's happening? The wolves are trying to weaken us. They want to subjugate us and conquer Zoon. We must stop it now. We must make sure the wolves never say a cruel word again."

There was much head nodding and agreement. The sheep looked around, expectant for another to speak. Snowy piped up. "How do we make them never say another cruel word?"

Over one hundred sheep watched their leader, waiting for her command. Tully thought for a second and then looked to the sky. Scores of gray pigeons zoomed to and fro above the pasture delivering messages. Right in the middle, three times the size of any pigeon, Owl jolted north to south in jagged, frantic lines. Since Tweed had commissioned him to find noteworthy news, the large-eyed bird had scoured Zoon for stories. He flew east till his wings ached and west till he dizzied but had found nothing. The land was peaceful and wholly uneventful, and a single glance to the sky communicated his desperation for any kind of scandalous story.

Tully stood on her hind legs and waved her front hooves. "Owl, come down here. I have news for you."

The bird plummeted out of the sky. He landed in the plush grass, and his talons sunk into the soft earth. "Where? When? Who?" His eyes were wide and bloodshot, and his neck lurched forward with every word. "What story? What happened? Tell me, tell me…come on, tell me."

"The wolves said mean mean things about us."

"What things? Violent things?"

"One day they might become violent. They said our wool coats were so soft the wind could tear them right off our skin. It was terribly mean and hurt our feelings a tremendous amount."

Owl tilted his head to the side and clucked his beak. "I don't understand. You want me to tell the citizens the wolves were mean to you? Why does the whole land need to know that?"

Tully rolled her eyes as though she wanted to bang her head against a rock. "This is no joking matter, Owl. It's hateful verbal abuse. Do you know what follows hatred? Violence, Owl, violence follows hatred. Do you want violence in Zoon?"

"No I don't want violence. That would be bad."

"You are correct, Owl, it would be very bad, very very bad. It would threaten Zoon and our citizens' freedoms. We don't want that do we?"

"No we don't want that at all." Owl twisted his neck around to survey the sky. "Give me five minutes. The wind is strong. I'll have to be loud." He beat his wings hard against the air and caught a fast breeze off the knoll.

His heart fluttered with excitement. He had waited days for his first official announcement. He knew once citizens heard his voice they would come to know his presence in the air. They would associate his voice with the proclamation of important information. And when that had occurred, he would have their undivided attention whenever and however he wished.

On the hill's western side, over Wolf Habitat, the words burst from his beak. "Attention, citizens, I have an announcement." The sudden tenor in the clouds snapped the citizens' eyes toward the sky. The voice had an urgent tone, as if whatever followed, whether trivial or paramount, was vital to well-being. "This morning a wolf made cruel remarks about sheep. The unprovoked and insensitive wolf said sheep coats were so soft the faintest wind gust could tear them off. Such remarks are hateful and unwarranted in Zoon Garden."

For a moment the land was quiet. No one made a peep as they digested the information. Ironpaw stood on a rock outcrop at the peak of his habitat, looking utterly confused. His face puckered like he had tasted spoiled meat. "Halfear, do you hear this? The sheep are crying over a pigeon comment."

The elder wolf stepped higher on the rock. "It appears someone hurt their feelings."

"Their feel...I hate them, Halfear, hate them."

"I told you, sir. They have strange ideas."

"It's not just their ideas." A tar black wolf, so dark he

blended with night, stepped to Ironpaw's opposite side. His irises were dark gray, and his fangs had a dark, reddish hue. His name was Darkfang, and he was the most zealous of the wolves. He would have suffered one thousand gruesome deaths for the pack. "It's their entire being. They are weak and insecure. They're bound to attack anyone who says something against them."

"Of course, anyone can see that," said Ironpaw. "But why do they need to announce it to everyone? No one cares."

"I think they want you to apologize," added Halfear.

Ironpaw leaned his head back aghast. "Apologize? They want me to apologize for a comment? The wolves probably said it as a joke."

"We don't even know if a wolf said it. But that doesn't matter. From Owl's tone I'd say they're demanding an apology."

Ironpaw's face contorted with disgust. "Halfear, I'm a reasonable citizen. But that's the stupidest, rudest, most preposterous accusation I have ever heard. I'll claw my own jugular before those sheep force me to apologize." Ironpaw threw his head back and howled, "Owl, you tell those bah-bahs it's the truth. It wouldn't take a gust of wind. A breath the wrong direction would slash their soft coats to pieces."

Owl's eyes bulged with excitement. "Ooo, this is good...good, good, good." He zoomed east to the pasture. "Attention citizens, the wolves believe the sheep, the 'bah-bahs' as they cruelly call them, are softer than first believed. They think a mere breath could tear their wool apart."

At this comment the land exploded with babble. Dramatized by Owl, the meager, meaningless announcement escalated to a monumental affair.

"That's terrible," someone shouted. "I have never heard something so hateful."

"Those sheep are overreacting. They're just words."

"You can't say things like that. Words are hateful. Words can kill."

"We are sheep, not bah-bahs!" Tully shrieked. "Owl, you tell those monsters to call us by our proper name!"

Isabella called Ironpaw "a heartless beast." Koalas threw nuts over the fence at the wolves. But Raka the cheetah did something no citizen foresaw. While he watched Owl circle above in his periphery, Raka called down a pigeon, wrapped his paw around the messenger and smiled. "Are you feeling brave today, little bird?"

"I guess so," peeped the pigeon, hesitation in its voice.

"Good. I need you to do something special for me. That owl should not have the only voice in our land. I want you to announce my message around Zoon so all the citizens can hear."

"I don't think that's allowed, sir," squeaked the small bird. "A pigeon has never done that."

"You can be the first. I'm sure you have a loud voice. Fly through the garden telling the citizens my message. Owl's voice will overpower yours, but for at least a moment the citizens will hear you."

"If you want, I can try."

"Good. That's all I ask. Listen, I want you to say…"

Within a few minutes the small pigeon lifted above the habitats. It settled at an elevation a hundred feet below Owl, who was now shouting about wolf oppression and sheep persecution. The pigeon shuddered at his sharp talons the size of its torso. Then it gained a spit of courage and heaved in air till its lungs felt fit to burst. "Citizens!" The noise came out a shrill tweet, but it was loud and sufficient. "Raka the cheetah believes the sheep are 'emotional citizens who make a great fuss out of a whole lot of nothing.'"

Owl darted down and chased the tiny pigeon away. But the deed was done. Everyone had witnessed a pigeon announce a normal citizen's message to the multitudes. The circular tower erupted into a madhouse. Birds entered and exited the countless holes every two seconds, squawking messages to one another. "Sharif says to announce…" "Isabella told me to say…" "Tully says we need to…"

"Announce them all!" the lead pigeon shouted perched on her center roost inside the tower, ordering her birds every direction. Excrement splattered the walls and roosts. Bags of feed spilled onto the wooden floor. Pigeons shot around her to the ceiling, to the floor, to the holes, avoiding crashes by centimeters. "Announce whatever they want. Faster, go, go, go, we're getting behind."

Now that a citizen had utilized a pigeon to promulgate personal belief, citizens believed they too had brilliant and foolproof opinions. Hundreds demanded their sentiments be shared to the multitudes just as Raka had. An influx of birds blanketed the sky in a hazy, gray blob like a polarized cloud, screeching the citizens' divided sentiments across the air for everyone to hear.

For the rest of the day hundreds of pigeons shot through the sky, Ironpaw howled from his rock cliff, Tully shrieked from her knoll, and Owl, furious the pigeons had tried to stifle his voice, flew fifty feet off the ground shouting loudest of all. In the chaotic blurb of polarized information the watchful citizens' heads spun in circles, clueless what to think, which to believe, or who to trust. It seemed in that cloud of opinions any citizen might be right, any citizen might be wrong, any might have genuine motivations, or any might have a clandestine agenda.

6

THE NEXT MORNING before anyone awoke, Tweed crept out of his habitat. The portly bear sneaked down the road past sleeping citizens, past the silent office, casting discreet glances at the mysterious building. It struck him as suspicious that neither Chimp nor the zookeeper had said nor done anything the previous day to quell the citizens' anger. Not a peep had come from the office. The gray stone building, lightless, quiet, and eerie, looked abandoned, and Tweed wondered why Chimp and the zookeeper were nowhere to be seen at such a contentious time.

He entered Maximus's habitat and scrambled onto the hill. With labored breaths he climbed the loose soil to the cave mouth as the sun peeked in the east. He knocked on the large rock outside the cave. "Good morning, Maximus, is this a good time? I know it's early."

No answer came. Overhead, veiling the fading starlight, the bird cloud continued to announce random sentiments, leftover remnants from the previous day's heated quarrels. At its peak the prior day, the cloud had covered a quarter of the sky. It was an efficient, continuous operation, and with the influx of citizens' opinions and growing pigeon population, Tweed thought it was likely to keep expanding.

He blinked his eyes away from the distracting cloud and knocked once more. "Maximus, are you awake? I can return later if necessary but now would be best. I have urgent business that requires your attention." He rubbed a smooth stone slab slung in the satchel around his neck. He had hovered chisel and hammer over the stone tablet through the night, trying to find the right phrases. The proper language was pivotal, he knew. The words had to be poignant yet ambiguous, crafted in a way in which Maximus would agree to ratification.

"Sir, I presume you're busy," he called a third time into the cave. "I'll return this afternoon."

"I am here," said Maximus, pulling his body over the ledge from the hillside behind Tweed. His fur was covered in faint road dust, and sinew jutted out of his neck.

"Ah, there you are, sir. An early walk today, I see."

"Longer than usual, many things to contemplate."

"I understand. Yesterday was a strange day."

"The strangest I have seen." He brushed past the black and white bear into the cave. Tweed shuffled inside after him. The bear's home was dark and cool and simple but dry and nonetheless welcoming. Maximus took a pawful of berries and offered some to Tweed. "Oh, no thank you. I ate before I came."

Maximus popped the berries in his mouth and sat on the floor. "Yesterday was madness."

"Complete madness."

"I never anticipated such incivility."

"It is their speech which concerns me most. They couldn't control their tongues. Rude names, demeaning accusations—they said terrible things to one another. For a few hours the citizens were savages."

"They were something, something concerning."

His face full of concern, Tweed stepped closer to the grizzly. "Citizens are supposed to be nice, not mean. A civilized land like ours should be a place of kindness, not hatred. We can't let this go on, Maximus. We must ensure our wild, uncultured citizens are restrained by more than their dull minds, because you know as well as I their consciences won't do it for them."

"What do you suggest?"

Tweed withdrew the stone slab and laid it at Maximus's feet. "Last night I wrote the First Decree of Zoon Garden."

Maximus slid the slab below his snout and ran his calloused paw over the surface. Deep, engraved words, two sentences worth, were etched into the hard rock in crisp, even lines. "You want to enact a law?"

"Precisely. We can't have our citizens saying what they want or how they feel; it may offend other citizens. This decree will limit hatred and obligate citizens to compassion and kindness. It will ensure our citizens say and do what others approve."

Maximus did not understand the desire for a decree. He had never seen a problem integrity could not fix, nor a law that fully solved any problem. But neither had he understood much of what he had seen in Zoon in recent weeks. The prior day's incessant bickering had been a hammer to his skull, and he was tired and perplexed, confused why citizens would act like children. But his duty, as he saw it, was to assure citizens were free to live the lives they wished. And whether he agreed with their decisions or not, these seemed to be the lives they desired.

"The citizens want this law? You spoke to them?"

"Yes," responded Tweed. "They desire decree protection."

"You are certain this is what they want?"

"Positive. I spoke with many of them last night."

Maximus looked at the decree once more, tracing his nail over the lines. He wondered what would be considered approved and appropriate conduct. Who would determine acceptable behavior? He had never heard of forced unity, or compelled kindness, or coerced empathy. He doubted the whole of society would ever agree on anything, and if they did, it would not be because they were forced to agreement by a law. Despite Tweed's smooth words, he disagreed with the proposal. But the decree implied any disagreement was prohibited.

Maximus looked up from the tablet. "Do you take me for a fool, Tweed?"

"Sir? Why would you say such a thing? You are our faithful and wise leader."

"You think I'm foolish enough to enact this decree. Any citizen can see this will cause chaos, not peace."

"Maximus, that is a pessimistic and inaccurate assumption! The First Decree will create an orderly land rid of hatred and full of kind conduct." Tweed rapped his knuckles hard on the stone. "Read the words, Maximus: 'Speech, actions, approved by all citizenry.' This will set us on a unified course. Besides, my bear friend, you well know it's not your place to critique; it's your job to grant citizens' requests. Now you would never deny your citizens' demands for sake of your own miscalculated worry, would you?"

Tweed paused for the grizzly's response, analyzing the brown, stoic face. Maximus detected the slightest sliver of a smirk on the panda's countenance, but it quickly vanished as Tweed continued. "I have told you twice now, Maximus, more than half your citizens, a significant and noteworthy majority, want this decree ratified. The sheep, the giraffes, the koalas, the armadillos, the peacocks, the prairie dogs—go speak with them yourself. Go ask Tully, go talk to Isabella. Don't take my word; go to them, hear your citizens' requests with your own ears."

"I heard them. Tully voiced her complaints." Maximus felt an engulfing desire to strike the panda. He knew Tweed had motives; everyone always had motives; the whole land was a game of motives. And the false presumption that he was blindly aloof of Tweed's ploys made him want to send the spotted bear hurtling down the hill. Yet he knew Tweed was right. That was the worst part; it was a leader's duty to grant his citizens' requests, no matter how blind or foolish they might be.

Maximus viewed the words a third time. He did not want to make his mark; he wanted to hurl the stone in a lake and watch it sink, watch the fish nibble it and the water drown it from memory. But these were not his choices. This was a land by and for the animals, and they would decide its course. "Very well," he said with a reluctant mutter. "Bring it near the puddle."

Tweed hustled the stone tablet near a murky puddle along the cave wall. Maximus stuck his paw in the water and hovered it over the slab, and as the knot quivered in his throat and mud globs dripped off his trembling claw, he pressed the muddy print into the center of Zoon Garden's First Decree.

Tweed's smile extended to his earlobes. "Well done, Maximus, well done. A triumphant day, a monumental event, we shall remember this for centuries. Our citizens will praise you for your lawful protection."

"I do not need their praise or my name ever mentioned. My duty is to honor the citizens' wishes."

"And you do it splendidly."

Maximus watched Tweed quickly tuck the decree into his satchel. "You'll have the other leaders make their marks?"

"Of course. Once marked, Owl will declare it. Then it will be an official law of our land." Tweed dipped his head and whisked out of the cave.

That afternoon Owl fluttered on a delicate breeze above Sheep Pasture. His body blocked the sun, projecting a black silhouette over the land. He remained furious over the pigeons' incessant background chatter, but, as there was nothing he could do to stop them, he was determined to shout louder to drown out the smaller birds. "Attention, citizens!" He was getting better. His choreographed arcs mesmerized the eye, and his oiled-tongue soothed the ear. "In response to yesterday's events, for your welfare, your faithful advocate Tweed has helped create the First Decree of Zoon Garden. From this day forward: Citizens must conduct their speech and actions in a manner approved by all citizenry. Terms of offense, ill words, or hurtful ideas shall not be tolerated."

7

TULLY DANCED THROUGH her pasture happier than she
had ever been. "Yes! Yes! Snowy, did you hear? Tell me
you heard. Oh, it's wonderful. Ill words and hurtful ideas have
been outlawed."

Snowy looked up from her afternoon grass snack. Joy spar-
kled in her eyes. "That means the wolves can't say any more
mean insults. That means no more hateful verbal abuse."

"Yes! It means both those things. Oh, this is a good day.
There will be peace, kindness, compassion, love." She could
hardly contain her enthusiasm. "Wonderful, this is wonderful!
It's a fantastic day to be a citizen." Tully ran through the field
to tell the other sheep the heartening news.

On the hill's opposite side, Halfear walked through the pine
tree forest alongside Ironpaw. The elder wolf seemed more
alarmed with each passing day. "I have a question for you," he
said, clearly concerned. "This decree, what is meant by our actions must be approved by all citizenry?"

Ironpaw's claws crunched the thin brown needles blanketed

over the forest floor. "I'm not sure. I've been asking myself the same. I suppose it means what it says: everyone must approve what everyone else says and does."

"What about hurtful ideas and terms of offense? Who gets to determine whether an idea is hurtful or a term offensive?"

"I suppose everyone."

Just at that moment, the older wolf's ears perked. Through the forest's canopy the bird cloud was growing louder with citizens' opinions.

Throughout the coming weeks, citizens watched the pigeons sweep through the sky. There was something alluring in the movement, the loud noises, the aesthetic spectacle, something that stimulated the senses; they could not help but watch the bird cloud. They soon realized pigeons could, loosely speaking, announce anything—wisdom, idiocy, gossip, logic, foolishness, bias, facts, or pure lies; it did not matter. If they were instructed, pigeons would repeat anything.

One by one citizens' thoughts entered the ether proclaiming what they believed. Koalas spoke of leisure and meditation, giraffes of pleasure and experience, cheetahs of individualism. Continuous chirpy squawking filled the sky, and citizens spent the majority of the day with necks tilted, eyes and ears glued to the network of ideas consuming the air.

Now this was all well and good, except for one insoluble problem: every idea, no matter how benign, hurt or offended someone. Wolves did not see koala leisure; they saw laziness, a proven poison to success. Beavers did not see giraffe pleasure; they saw boorish behavior, a threat to traditional ethics. Sheep did not see cheetah individualism; they saw refusal to conform, an intrinsic danger to unification. And with the advent of law that expressly stated: "Citizens must conduct their speech, as well as actions, in a manner approved by all citizenry," citizens now had legal encouragement, even an obligation, to report anyone who acted, spoke or thought in a manner they disapproved.

Tweed stood inside his home, polishing the First Decree. The house was modest: red tin roof, wooden slat walls, no more than twenty by twenty feet. Inside, a cozy bed pad nestled against the left wall, plush seat cushions formed a tight circle in the center for visitors, and shelves lined the home's edges, packed full of tightly rolled records sealed with bamboo clasps. An additional inch of blubber, courtesy of pre-winter gorging, shook as Tweed's paw swished the varnish-soaked cloth over the stone till the surface reflected his smiling face. He was busy watching his own reflection in the shiny stone when a swift clatter rapped on the door, not the hard clobber of a hoof or paw, more like a quick whip. "Come in," Tweed said without taking his eyes off his reflection. "Door is open."

A snake's nose nudged the door. It wriggled between the frame and the door but struggled to swing it open. The tongue flicked in and out through the gap. "Pardon, a little help."

"Apologies, one moment." Tweed hurried across the room and opened the door the rest of the way. The snake slithered inside, slicing a swiveled trail in the dirt behind him. His skin was three shades of brown with black splotches along the back, sleek and smooth, like he had shed two days prior. He had a diamond-shaped skull, and his tail, erect behind his head, twitched and rattled as he moved. He slithered to the center of the room and coiled into a tight ball.

"My apologies again for the door," said Tweed, setting aside his polishing cloth. "Please, here, you look exhausted." Tweed offered the snake a cushion. He slid onto the seat and coiled back into a tight ball. Tweed sat down across.

"I am exhausted." The snake's thin, forked tongue flicked out and sucked back in. "Your home is a long distance to sssssslither from Sssssnake Habitat."

"You slithered all this way? You should have sent a pigeon."

"You're right. But this is different." His onyx-black eyes flashed behind double lenses. "I knew I had to come to you."

Tweed leaned forward on the cushion. "Has something happened?"

The snake coiled tighter, as though stabbed with physical pain. "I'm afraid the sssssstory I have to tell is perhaps worse than anything you have heard. Yesterday I witnessed a frightful First Decree violation committed by the ostriches."

"Did they call you a foul name?"

"Worse." His rattle quivered faster above his head. "Much worse. As you know, Ostrich Habitat borders my own on the north sssssside. Our largest rocks are near there. Needless to sssssay, three weeks ago, five of us sssssoaked sssssunrays on those rocks. It was a bright day as you might remember. I closed my eyes to block the light, and that's when I heard them. Two ostriches whispered near the fence. These are the exact words I heard. Write them if you wish." Tweed quickly grasped for parchment and pencil. "The ostrich sssssaid, 'Sssssnakes deserve nothing. What sssssort of important citizen lacks legs?'"

Tweed bore hard into the parchment. "That is terrible. This

is a clear violation."

"I thought sssssso. It was hurtful, offensive, and the sssssnakes certainly don't approve. I wanted your confirmation."

"You have my full confirmation." Tweed scribbled harder. "This is shameful. I can't believe a citizen would say such a thing."

"That's only one of the nasty things I've heard ostriches sssssay. And they make the pigeons sssssay cruel things too."

"I can only imagine. It is a shame. Rest assured, I will handle this matter."

"Thank you, Tweed. You are a fine leader." Satisfied his complaint would be well handled, the snake slithered toward the exit. Tweed held open the door and saw him onto the road. The air had a nippy bite, and Tweed's frosted breath billowed in the morning glow.

"I was next if you're ready for me," a voice stated. Startled, Tweed jumped and spun around at the sudden sound. A zebra, evidently flustered, stood in front of his house ten feet from the door. "I got here first, but that stupid snake skipped the line. Snakes are rude like that."

Tweed glanced behind her. Thirty, forty, maybe even fifty, it was hard to count, citizens stood in queue. "Did you all witness First Decree violations?"

Every head nodded. "Very well." Tweed looked at the zebra. "Please come in."

As the day dragged on, the queue outside Tweed's door grew longer and longer. Sometime around noon it broke one hundred and kept climbing. Tweed was diligent with each citizen, writing down the violation, doing his best to empathize, and, until half past midnight, maintaining eye contact. He stayed awake well into the morning working through three additional rolls of parchment, two pencils, and one cramped paw near arthritic by dawn.

Like most things in the land, the reported violations were eclectic. Multiple sheep complained about wolf ferocity and hatred. Five giraffes contended beavers "shamed anyone who wanted to have a good time." "Weak-willed koalas" offended two wolves. And a chameleon complained he overheard an otter call him "multi-skinned." Practically any word spoken or action taken had offended a citizen and thereby violated the First Decree.

By dawn, Tweed compiled the various parchments and paper scraps spread across his floor into a succinct violation list. At nine o'clock sharp Owl flew into the center of the sky with the list clutched in his talon and launched into an accusatory broadcast. "Attention, citizens, it has come to our leaders' attention that the land has suffered a plethora of First Decree violations. Citizens should take these violations seriously. We will not stand for hatred. Those who spread ill words and hurtful ideas will be reprimanded.

"The following citizens violated the First Decree: One. Ozzie the ostrich suggested snakes should lose citizenship because they lack legs. Two. Sid the snake said Ostrich eggs are ugly and abnormal. Three. Imani the monkey continues to call flamingos 'foo-foos.' Four. Jonesy the cheetah referred to sloths as 'breathing infestations.' Five. Sharif the giraffe…"

The violations continued for half an hour. At the end every

species in some respect had accused and been accused of a First Decree violation. Every single citizen in the garden, in one way or another, violated the First Decree purely by being alive.

Between offended citizens and Owl's eyes perpetually on the prowl, nothing stayed secret in Zoon for long. Minuscule frustrations inflated. The slightest paw out of line was reported. It became a Zoonian pastime to focus on minor actions, even events from the distant past, to spot violators, and to afterward humiliate them. Citizens came to Tweed with extensive complaints, and, to gain their support, he always found a way for the First Decree to accommodate. Zoon transformed into a verbal battle armed with catapults of violation and arrows of accusation with final goals to slander other citizens.

Citizens soon anticipated hurtful violations. Boundaries of offense sprouted. Misplaced looks became offensive. Random bypassing comments became attacks. The citizens were so offended by the slightest erroneous breath that they found other citizens' every word or action carried a hint of assault. Difficult ideas could not be discussed without immediate criticism. Candid conversations lasted only seconds before someone was insulted.

Violation Silence, this newest Zoon phenomenon, gained such an entrenched foothold that the citizens became constrained to follow a strict, unwritten list of approved subjects, phrases, and ideas. "Bah-bah," was deemed an offensive expletive never to be spoken. Reference to an adult wolf as a "monster" was also outlawed. No one knew who controlled the list, or even admitted the list existed, but new words and topics appeared on the unwritten banishment list every day, and hardly anyone could keep track of what they were permitted to say or do.

Citizens were uncertain what exploit or expression or even inclination of an expression might garner a pigeon from an angry citizen or land their name on Owl's shame list. So they kept quiet, hesitant to word or action, quite uncertain what opinions were permissible, and in the end decided it best to keep mouths sealed shut lest they incur citizenry contempt. The silence, however, had no impact on thoughts. The First Decree suppressed words and actions with ostracism, but as hard as it tried, it never accomplished its intentions; it never blotted thoughts; it never changed minds; it never crafted compassionate hearts. It created frustrated citizens like shushed red-faced toddlers. The decree's discouragement of dialogue elevated animosities and forced potent enmities inside where they boiled and boiled and boiled.

8

RAKA AND JONESY tramped through five-foot-tall grass; they now knew better than to talk out in the open. Their bodies blended with the tan fibers, and aside from the occasional rustle or angry shout, the cheetahs were hidden in the grass.

Raka swatted a stalk away from his face. "These bah-bahs are driving me mad, brother. I thought they would be quiet like everybody else, but noooo, the sheep make everyone else be quiet, yet they yell louder. Why do they keep targeting us with decree violations? What on earth did we do to them?"

Jonesy slid his slender body through the tanned grasses. "Those fluffy bah-bahs think we urinate in the wrong spot, eat in the wrong manner; goodness, Raka, they think we breathe the wrong way."

"Right! Everyt—"

"Quiet, quiet. Owl will hear if you talk too loud."

Raka quieted to an almost inaudible whisper. "Everything we do or say is hateful to them; it's as if our very existence hurts them. Before we know it they will have us sleeping when they tell us and eating when they let us. And, brother, they laugh because they know they control us."

"The bah-bahs are a disease. They contaminate the mind."

"You hear that, bah-bahs," Raka stood on his hind paws and shouted to the sky, "you're a disease!"

Jonesy slapped a paw over his brother's snout. "What happened to quiet?"

Raka smirked through his brother's claw. "I had to make sure everyone knew."

Jonesy chuckled and shoved his head. "Trust me, brother, they are well aware. But, in seriousness, what are we to do? The reason the sheep hate everything we do—it's perfectly obvious really—is because they're determined to turn us all into sheep. They want all citizens to be part of their flock, to walk like them, talk like them, and behave how they approve. And I'll tell you right now, Raka, look at me, look at me." The younger cheetah turned. Jonesy's face was stern and his wide, yellow eyes were mirthless. "I am not becoming a sheep."

"Never. I would let them hang me on a branch by my tail before I followed Tully. I tell you what, Jonesy, I would love to get my claws on one of those bah-bahs. Teach them a lesson or two."

"Don't let them hear you say that. Owl will call you violent and dangerous."

"Of course not. All citizens must be quiet; all citizens must obey." Raka winked at his brother. "I am concerned though, Jonesy. The sheep are Zoon's greatest threat. Imagine it—a land run by bah-bahs…what could be worse?"

"Nothing. It's the worst thing possible, worse than sloths." The cheetahs reached the edge of the grass near the watering hole. The small cheetah clan lay around the muddy spring in the shade of a small grove. "We need to warn the citizens. We need to make them aware. If we do nothing, before we know it we'll all be baying and eating dandelions."

In the following days, as November drew near, the brothers spoke ill of the sheep in inner circles and hidden places outside of Owl's earshot. Many citizens listened to them; and cheetahs, along with wolves, snakes, monkeys and others, began to believe in the legitimate danger of a land ruled by soft fluffy sheep.

One November morning, Owl's screeching voice blasted across the sky. He sounded frightened and frantically flapped his wings. "Citizens! Citizens! There has been an attack in Sheep Pasture. An attack! A physical attack! A sheep is on the ground and bleeding." Prairie dog heads popped out of holes. Buffalos stopped chewing mid chomp. Owl's pupils tapered. He arced back around, peering into the grass valley. "The victim has cuts on its legs and back. White wool crimson. Blood everywhere."

In the pasture Tully pressed grass compresses against the victim's body, as others ran to gather more bandages. "Stop squirming. I need to stop the bleeding." The victim winced against the pressure. The gouges were deep. Blood oozed into the matted wool, but with pressure the flow was slowing. Tully forced the grass deeper into the wound. "What happened? Who did this? Where are they?"

The sheep squirmed and grimaced against the compression. "I don't know, ma'am. It crept behind me. I didn't see it. I didn't hear it till it was too late. I tried to run. Oh, Tully, I ran as fast as I could, but it was so fast, so fast, I closed my eyes and…"

The sheep's breath was quickening.

Snowy dabbed her head with moist moss. "There, shhh, it's over. You're safe now."

Tully pressed the bandages harder. Her hooves trembled against the sheep's body. "I said stop squirming. Was it a cheetah? Sounds like a cheetah. What did it look like?"

The sheep writhed in pain but tried to keep still. "I don't know. It happened so fast."

"How can you not know? The beast attacked you."

"I was scared. I closed my eyes. It leaped on my back, and when I opened my eyes, it was gone."

Tully's white ears turned scarlet, and blood vessels swelled on her forehead. She motioned for another sheep to hold the bandages and rounded on the flock. "I told you! I said it! Did you not listen? Did you not believe me? It always escalates to violence. Always!" The leader shook with wrath, furious she had been powerless to prevent the attack. "We're lucky she's alive. Spread out. Go in groups of five. It must be a cheetah, nothing else is that fast. Search the pasture, secure the fences, make sure it's off our land."

Overhead, Owl delivered his newest update. "Citizens, I have just learned a cheetah attacked the sheep. The cat snuck into the pasture and mauled the innocent citizen. I repeat: a cheetah attacked the sheep."

At this moment, Eagle stood in her nest and unfurled her wings. After the Day of Freedom, she had built a new home in the highest boughs of the tallest tree and had intended to live out her days alone in her peaceful nest. High in the tree, however, she could not help but see the land's events. She found the recent ordeals chaotic on all fronts, but no one infuriated her more than Owl. She felt neither jealousy nor rivalry, nor anything of the sort; she simply hated the bird. His constant blabber annoyed her, and everything he said she thought foolish and misinformed. In her eyes he had grown progressively biased in the sheeps' favor, and this unverified cheetah accusation was her final straw.

Eagle's talons snapped the twigs in her nest as she adjusted for flight. Her wings, each three-feet long and brown with hints of grey, flapped as the wind submitted. She plunged after Owl.

Oblivious to his surroundings, the large-eyed bird continued to yell as he scanned the ground. "No telling where the violent attacker is now. Citizens, be on the lookout for a bloodstained cheetah sneaking back to his habitat. Inform me right away if the violent beast is spotted."

Eagle hurtled past Owl, sending him spinning through the air. "Citizens, don't listen to Owl. He doesn't tell you the truth. A cheetah has not been confirmed as the attacker."

Fazed for a moment, disoriented from sudden shock, Owl recovered and flew past her screeching louder. "Eagle is a liar. A cheetah attacked an innocent sheep!"

Eagle swooped around behind him. "Leave the sky, you stupid fowl. No one needs to hear your foolish opinions."

"No, you leave. I was here first." Owl darted past her to a lower elevation and continued to shout about cheetah attackers.

Both birds, too arrogant to yield, flew in circles under each other—hopeful the lower they flew the better the citizens would hear their voice. Sometimes they bumped each other out of the way. On occasion one went east and the other west, but usually they stayed in the center side by side trying to out yell the other.

In the subsequent days, more information came to light. Everyone knew cheetahs despised the sheep—any cheetah would have told them so. But Raka swore none of his cheetahs had attacked anyone. According to him, none had left the habitat at that specific time and none had been seen covered in blood. Tully, however, studied the gouges and bite marks and further questioned the victim. The wounds matched. The story's details aligned. She was absolutely certain a cheetah had committed the atrocity, and the more the cheetahs denied guilt, the angrier she became. She began to believe more and more that the predatory citizens, led by the wolves, were trying to covertly dominate the land.

Meanwhile Eagle and Owl continued to bicker in the sky. One yelled, "sheep wrongly accuse innocent cheetahs," while the other shouted, "dangerous cheetahs viciously attack innocent sheep." Citizens, of course, never saw the actual events. They were entirely at the mercy of the birds in the sky to convey reality. And depending on which bird they listened to, they learned a different story. Attention bounced from Owl to Eagle and Eagle to Owl, uncertain whom to believe.

After days of bitter squabbling, they never confirmed who or what attacked the sheep citizen. Yet Tully swore it was a cheetah; and Raka swore the sheep had framed him.

However it did not matter who had attacked or what had motivated the perpetrator; citizens were scared, anxiety had grown, and no one could comprehend why a Zoon citizen would attack another citizen. They were afraid to go outside, worried to be alone, and fearful a savage citizen would jump out of the bushes and make them the next helpless victim bleeding in the grass.

Supported by hundreds of citizens and compelled by supposed compassion to guarantee another atrocious attack would never occur, Tully met with Tweed and Maximus. She demanded something be done to assure Zoon citizens' safety. "This is a land of peace," she argued. "Violence of any nature should not exist in the garden. An armadillo should never feel afraid while eating dinner. An otter should not fear an attack while playing with his pups."

Maximus agreed with her intentions; even Raka and Ironpaw agreed. But they were less enthusiastic about her solution. The wolves and cheetahs tried to argue against it, calling it too drastic, radical, unfair. But discussions quickly escalated to fiery quarrels, and after an hour, wolves and sheep were cursing and slandering about "bah-bah radicalism" and "monster selfishness." Ironpaw and Raka stormed out of the meeting, and Tully's Second Decree of Zoon Garden passed by a large majority.

Tweed chose the language and chiseled the stone. Owl promulgated the law across the land. "No citizen shall bear fangs or claws or any implement which could physically harm another citizen."

The next afternoon grass-woven gloves and muzzles were issued to the populace. Every cheetah, wolf, snake and bear was mandated to glove their paws and muzzle their mouth, lest their innate violent tendencies tempt them to hurt citizens.

9

I N AN ACT of defiance, scores of predatory citizens vehemently refused the infernal gloves and mandatory muzzles. They proudly marched through their habitats, bearing their fangs, flexing their claws, yelling about the growing threat of "sheep tyranny."

Ironpaw yelled, marching at the head of the protestors. "First our voices, now our bodies...this is what happens when the bah-bahs lead. What else will these sheep take from us? Down with the sheep! Down with the freedom-stealing bah-bahs!"

The demonstrations incited considerable fear amongst the sheep populace. They found the protests aggressive and intimidating and fretted over the potential of more attacks. There were additional complaints, and the following day, Maximus, looking none too thrilled but with his head held high, walked down the asphalt road past the protesting predators, humbly wearing his own muzzle and gloves.

"Look at him," someone sneered.

"Whose side is he on anyhow?"

"He's turning into a bah-bah lover."

There were many whispers of Maximus's apostasy and even talk that he had become a full-fledged sheep ally. Yet the predators, some out of fear, others out of respect, trudged back to their homes and begrudgingly strapped on their muzzles and cinched up their gloves, removing them only to eat or drink. The restrictive gloves snagged wherever they walked; the muzzles chaffed their snouts and made it hard to speak or sniff. Raka hated every minute of it. Ironpaw vowed it would not stay this way for long. And both the cheetahs and the wolves became fully convinced the sheep were on a subliminal mission to control Zoon and make every citizen speak, behave, and live like sheep.

Maximus tried his best to pretend his own muzzle and gloves were comfortable, but he too hated his new restraints. There was much he did not understand and much more that troubled him. Silence worried him. The bird cloud that at times covered half the sky concerned him. The new decrees terrified him. He missed the days when life was simpler, when a citizen could wake in the morning and make sense of what he saw in the day. He knew not what would happen next or what else would come, but he felt a sense of impending chaos and wondered why the land around him felt in a spiral of decline. He lacked facts or preconceived knowledge to cite, and part of him thought he was a pessimist. But he had hunches from the air, the trees, the dirt, the places from whence he came and to which he would return. He watched them and they told him many things, not in words but in movements and instincts and premonitions, and he trusted those primordial forces more than the mortal creatures that spoke of what they knew.

Since Tweed's meeting Maximus had spent extensive time considering what he should do. He wanted to act. He wanted to do something to quell the escalating disorder. But what could he do? The land was not his; he was a reflection of the citizens. The land belonged to them, and they wanted it this way. Intervention would be obstruction, forced mandates an act of repression. He thought to speak to the leaders and reason with them, but the recent events told him his words would fall on deaf ears.

Nevertheless, if he were to attempt to quell the swelling confusion, he needed to know why these events were happening. Why or what or who was causing the citizens to act this way? He needed answers. And he knew where to find them. If they lay anywhere, they lay in the hands of the zookeeper. But Chimp had barred that avenue and vehemently guarded the secret behind the office's door.

Before the zoo was freed, the office and the zookeeper were common discussion topics amongst the citizens. Though they never saw the zookeeper, there was a certain sense of intrigue surrounding him. The idea of a man, presumed intelligent, sitting at a desk in the office behind tinted bar-covered windows who, for some unknown reason, refused to reveal himself fascinated and frightened the citizens. They wondered what he might look like: his height, weight, the shade of his skin, the color of his eyes, blue or green or brown, or could they be the orange of molten magma? Where did he come from? Why was he so infinitely difficult to locate? Was he even a man? And more than any other question: what did he do all day behind that bolted door?

The potentials were limitless, and nothing had been confirmed outside Chimp's brief testimonies. Every few months, a
bold citizen had mustered enough courage to ask to speak with
the zookeeper or even to see a glimpse of him. But Chimp
skirted the requests with calculated remarks: "The zookeeper is
busy;" "He's gone at the present moment;" "I haven't seen him
in weeks." Patient citizens had waited a few days, asked again,
and received another calculated answer. This process continued
numerous times—as many as were needed it appeared—until
even the most stubbornly patient and obstinate citizens let the
zookeeper and his office remain a mystery only Chimp could
interpret.

But that was many seasons ago. No one had seen Chimp or
the zookeeper in a long time. And other than Maximus and
Tweed, hardly anyone had thought of the two mysterious individuals.

In the fourth week of November, Maximus sat on his ledge
and watched the office, thinking how he could avoid Chimp's
elusive remarks and approach the zookeeper. The windows remained dark and the façade barren of activity. Maximus felt the
place looked more like a ghost's haunt than a home for two. The
thought crossed his mind that Chimp might have left the office
or left the zoo altogether. He made a motion to start down the
hill toward the building when suddenly, to the far right of the
eastern chimney, he noticed an old wooden chest in the road. It
was worn and faded with a golden latch. Mystic designs covered
the veneer, and the seams were airtight. Maximus looked for a
citizen, the zookeeper, Chimp himself, anyone that could have

placed the chest, but it just sat in the dirt with nothing around it, as though it had been dug up from the depths of the earth.

He had never noticed it, and in fact he was almost positive it had not been there five minutes before. Somehow it had appeared, and he wondered if anyone else had seen it. This thought had hardly left his mind when Ironpaw suddenly peeked his nose into the road.

Crouched low, the wolf approached the chest, trying to sniff it from afar, but his muzzle dulled the scent. He crept closer. Then more curious citizens crawled out from behind the fences, intrigued but hesitant to go near. Ironpaw circled the ornate box. He flicked it with his paw then whipped it with his tail, but it stayed as dead as the dirt beneath it. Maximus saw him look backward then the wolf closed his eyes, gulped, and with a quick flick flung open the sealed chest.

Three hundred yards away Maximus felt a gust of wind burst through the land. He opened his eyes and saw Ironpaw standing over the chest, fur disheveled by the wind, rainbow light dancing on his face. Thousands of pristine objects—blue, yellow, indigo, periwinkle, shrouded with spots and spirals and prisms—filled the chest to the brim. It was difficult to determine the material. The objects looked denser than plastic, lighter than metal, and more manufactured than stone. Size varied from sand granules to small marbles, and the brighter the sun shone the brighter they glistened.

At the sight of the treasures, Tully and the other citizens rushed into the road. They crowded round the wolf and gazed over his shoulder. "What are they?" muttered Snowy.

"They are tiny beautiful beads," said Tully, engrossed by the twinkling trinkets.

Ironpaw dipped his gloved paw into the colorful depths and rolled the beads around. He lifted them, and everyone watched them cascade from his paw back into the chest. Then he suddenly slammed the lid shut. He tried to bark through his muzzle, but it came out a muffled growl. "Halfear, help me carry this back."

"What are you doing?" snapped Tully.

Ironpaw looked at her contemptuously as one does a cockroach he may soon decide to squash. "You can't take them all," she yapped. "You must share them." Ironpaw continued to leer, neither flinching nor blinking, breathing difficultly through the taut muzzle cinched around his snout. Tully stomped her hooves. "I know you hear me; it's your mouth that's covered not your ears. You must share the beads with everyone."

The silver-pawed wolf ground his teeth. "You just want to control everything, don't you?" Without waiting for a response, he turned to the wolves and helped Halfear drag the chest back to Wolf Habitat.

In the subsequent weeks leading into winter, the wolves hardly shared the beads with anyone. Cheetahs and select allies received portions, but the majority of the population failed to receive a single one. And to make matters worse, the wolves flaunted the beads. They hung the blood red ones with snow-colored speckles above their caves, and glued the sunflower yellow ones with kumquat stripes on their fences. Everyday citizens walked by and coveted the wolves' treasures, and the more Tully watched, the angrier she became.

10

OVER THE SPRING and summer, wolves lorded the beads over the populace, and their habitat became grander by the day. With each passing month citizens grew angrier over bead disproportion. Tully spoke of inequality and oppression, and though much of the citizenry had ignored her for many seasons, her messages started to resonate. Proud citizens began to feel disparaged by unjust, corrupt wolves.

Maximus rushed around the land in an effort to ease the heightening tensions. He managed small compromises and stifled little quarrels, but the zoo around him continued to unravel. Pigeons were squawking, animosities were flaring, and everywhere he looked someone was blaming someone else for this or that or life itself. He beseeched Tully to speak with Ironpaw but was met by shouts, "Don't tell me what I need to do, Maximus. It's their fault; they're the problem. Those selfish, dangerous, uncultured monsters started all of this." And when he spoke to Ironpaw, he was met with a similar response. "You want me to meet with her? Why? So she can slap chains on my ankles? Or does she want to put blinders on my eyes? Maximus, look around you—the muzzles, the gloves, the decrees. Don't be deceived by their kind words and compassionate causes. They're playing you for a fool. They want to eradicate citizens like you and I."

The harder Maximus tried to fix the worsening problems the more disillusioned he grew. He became very quiet and took to spending days at a time alone in his cave, trying to think of a way to reverse the land's direction.

At the beginning of the next fall, a full nine months later, tempers were rife. Half the animals were fed up with Zoon's direction and ready to take drastic measures to right these unequivocal wrongs. Tully ordered an urgent meeting for citizens disgusted by wolf oppression. Giraffes, koalas, prairie dogs, flying squirrels, and a whole assortment of citizens flooded into her pasture. When she thought the wave had settled, more citizens poured in until half the population stood in the pasture teeming with resentment.

Tully climbed atop a boulder over them. A hush covered the crowd. "Equality! It is a word which means all citizens are the same. All citizens should own the same land and have the same food regardless of their species. We want an equal world, but some citizens believe in domination and greed. I saw that chest. You saw it too. It had thousands of beads, more than enough for every citizen, and those selfish wolves stole them all right out from under our noses!"

"It's unfair," yelped a koala. "Wolves should not have a mountain of beads while we have none."

"If all are equal, all should receive an equal amount of

beads," insisted an armadillo.

"It's evil," shouted Sharif. "Ironpaw will oppress us till we're squashed under his paw."

The whole assembly started shouting and jumping. Isabella raised her long neck high above the crowd. "We will make the wolves give us their beads. They can't stop us all!"

The vigor and excitement suddenly stopped. All was quiet in the pasture, as fear swallowed the enthusiasm. Fangs and claws or not, wolves were formidable. They were fast, strong, and tenacious; no one wanted to fight them.

Everyone was silent. Then a young prairie dog, barely a foot tall, bent down in the grass and picked up a stone. She rolled it over in her smooth paw, flexing her fingers against the rigid surface. She tossed it to her other paw and practiced a throwing motion. "Beads for all," she said.

"What was that?" asked Isabella.

"I said, 'Beads for all!' Down with the wolves!"

"Aye!" Isabella lifted her head back over the crowd. "You heard her. Beads for all! Down with the wolves!" Fists flew in the air. Hooves stomped on the ground. Citizens picked up sticks and rocks, and yells of rage echoed in the valley. With Tully at the head, hundreds of angry citizens marched into the road toward Wolf Habitat.

A mile away, Ironpaw's ears perked up. He heard soft patter echo from the east like the first drum of thunder in a darkening sky. He sprinted to an overhanging rock and saw the protestors marching down the road. A feral howl burst from his throat, "At attention! Everyone into formation. Those stupid bah-bahs are headed toward our door."

The thirty wolves, male and female, young and old, rushed out of the pine trees and caves down the slopes into the field ten yards from the habitat's entrance. "Six across! Five deep!" Ironpaw shoved and pulled wolves, attempting to organize a defensive formation. They had seldom practiced any form of battle strategy. The youngest were clueless. The oldest tripped over paws and bumped into bodies. Ironpaw pushed the wolves into order. "Tighten up. Shoulder to shoulder."

It took more than a minute of commands and shoves before the pack stood abreast in a haphazard but compact formation. Faces were calm but minds restless; the less composed shook with anticipation as the distant chants rang louder. "Beads for all! Beads for all!"

Ironpaw paced up and down the formation tapping paws into a line. "Remember, they are weak, and you are wolves. We don't wish for bloodshed, but if those sheep are foolish enough to attack, we would be wise to end their foolishness." Ironpaw sprinted around the formation and then settled in the front. Hooves beat the asphalt like war drums. Tully marched the indignant horde toward Wolf Habitat. "Beads for all! Beads for all!"

Halfear stood beside Ironpaw. He was stoic and ready for what might come. "I must ask, bah-bah or not, is it wise to kill a citizen?"

Ironpaw scratched the muzzle strapped around his snout. He knew if he needed he could rip it off with ease. "I was brave enough to open that chest. They cowered and came running when they saw what was inside. This equality Tully preaches is not equality. And the only thing worse than false equality is forced equality. She silenced our tongues, muzzled our mouths, and now she wants to steal our property. Let her die for what she believes." Ironpaw sniffed the air and waited.

The habitat's steel entrance boomed with a loud, metallic slam. It boomed again and again and then swung open. Tully stood on the other side with six hundred citizens at her back. "Wolves, you have oppressed your fellow citizens long enough. We deserve equality. We are here to claim our rightful beads."

Ironpaw dug his gloved hind paws into the dirt and leaned forward. "Rightful? In this land you get what you earn."

"That's not fair," shouted Snowy from behind Tully.

"I believe that's the quintessence of fair," barked Ironpaw.

"No it's not. Equality is fair."

Ironpaw smirked beneath his muzzle. "I'll tell you what, little bah-bah. Let us see how equal we are. If you want your beads, come and take them." Snowy looked at Tully. Twenty yards away Ironpaw's tail twitched back and forth. "Come on now, let's see your bravery. I won't even tear off this muzzle you made me wear." Snowy's eyes jerked toward the ground and then she shuffled behind a zebra. "Loud mouth, dull bite. And what about you, sheep leader, will you show me how equal we are? One step, just one step toward me, that's all I need."

Tully hesitated. She looked at Isabella. The giraffe dropped her head and poked the grass. She looked for other sheep, but they were hiding in the crowd. She turned back to Ironpaw. "There is no need to fight today."

"Says she who brought a violent rebellion to my habitat."

"Give us what we want, and there will be no violence."

"Citizens earn their worth in this land. That is why it's equal.

You get nothing from us; you get nothing from me."

At that moment, Tully wished she had been born bigger, faster, with sharp claws and teeth. Nevertheless she was no timid sheep; she was ready to die for equality. And she knew the citizens at her back were too; they just needed a reminder. "I won't be intimidated by a wolf!" she shouted loud enough for her followers to hear. She stepped her right hoof into the habitat.

Ironpaw's smirk turned to a wide grin. His left paw stepped forward. Tully dug her hooves into the soil. Ironpaw lowered his haunches. Tully lowered her head.

Suddenly the wolf ranks flinched. Wait, it was a shuffle, a quick shuffle to the side to make way. Something was moving down the center. In domino effect the wolf ranks began to part. "Move out the way," someone yelled in the back. Wolves bumped one another out of the way with grumbles and questions, as they retreated on either side. Then they saw and turned silent and bowed their heads.

Maximus was walking down the center. His black nostrils flared in rhythm with his steps. His brown eyes kept their mark. His canines flashed beneath his muzzle.

"What are you doing? Don't do this," pleaded Ironpaw. "Don't be a fool."

Maximus walked straight past him, shifting neither left nor right, dead set on the rebellious citizens. Everyone wanted to flee, but the crowd was too tight. Those in the back had yet to realize the horror. Sharif tried to step over citizens. Snowy pissed where she stood.

Powerless to retreat, Tully bowed her head to the earth, and her drooping ears kissed the grass. Maximus stood over her, his hot breath like fire-lit steam blowing on her neck. She saw the massive paws in her periphery, wide and locked into the grass and capable, she knew, of untold damage. His teeth gnashed behind his muzzle, and the claws dug into the earth through the mesh gloves. There was one sniff, then more ragged breaths.

Tully suddenly heard a loud jostle, a deep exhale, and a soft thud. Then the breath stopped. The heavy steps began again. Tully raised her head enough to peek. Maximus was passing back through the broken ranks. The wolves' eyes pleaded for an explanation. Their mouths' begged to shout out. But no one dared question the alpha of Zoon Garden. Six inches from Tully's face lay a colossal cloth bag, half the wolves' entire bead collection.

11

IRONPAW'S BODY QUIVERED with rage. He watched the grizzly walk back through a hole in the fence toward his cave atop the hill. Every ounce of muscle fiber held his tongue from howling and his paws from thrashing. He would have challenged him, but Maximus was faster, bigger, and stronger. He was the alpha, and every citizen, even those who loathed it, submitted to the alpha.

Mouths hung agape. Some wolves stared at the hole where the betrayer had disappeared. Others ogled at the bead bag planted at Tully's feet.

"Forget him," snarled Ironpaw. "Back into formation."

The pack snapped back to order. Ironpaw stepped to the center and rounded on Tully. "Leave the beads where they are, and I won't hurt you."

Tully sniffed the bag and prodded it with her hoof. "What can you do, Ironpaw? Our leader has spoken."

"I'll hunt you down. I'll kill you if I need to."

"Murder? How brash of you."

"Give us back our beads, thief."

"These are not yours. They were given to us all and you self-ishly took them." Tully slid her nose under the cloth and pushed it up her snout. She braced her legs and heaved the bag onto her head. Wobbling under the enormity, she tottered to the left, then made an adjustment to the right, and then she settled. "My dearest wolves, I wish you a wonderful day."

Ironpaw rushed her. He churned through the earth, dirt flying behind him, gaining five feet, ten feet, twenty—a wolf dove and clipped his back leg. More wolves tackled him to the ground. He bucked his head and threw two of them off, but three more piled on. He howled, trying to toss them off his back. "Let me go. That bear is blind, but I see what she's doing. We can't let her get away with this."

Tully sneered and dug a divot in the wet earth. "You're powerless in this land, Ironpaw. You will always be second to Maximus."

A blood-curdling howl ripped from Ironpaw's throat. He hurled four wolves off his back, and kicked two more off his ankles. He charged her again. His legs fired like pistons, and spittle flew from his muzzled mouth.

Ten wolves leaped and heaved their full weight upon him. "She isn't worth it," one cried, clawing Ironpaw's eyes, yanking out his hair, biting his ears to slow him. "She's devious. She wants you angry." Ironpaw took two more steps with the load on his back and collapsed under the weight. Pinned on his chest, he wildly flung his head and tried to snap his jaws. "Get off me. She'll steal freedom. She'll destroy everything."

Tully smirked and turned around. The crowd divided to

make a path. The crowned sheep walked through them, and the citizens clapped their hooves in applause. They filed in behind her to be first in line for their portion of promised beads.

That night, under the moonlight, the citizens threw a feast in Sheep Pasture. Delicious odors wafted across land, and dancing and laughter and merriment broke out. Tully's followers were immeasurably grateful for her bravery. Koalas hugged her, peacocks thanked her, and the citizens cheered when Tully gave them each three beads.

On the opposite side of the hill, the wolves cringed at the sounds of celebration. Ironpaw sat under the pine trees with seven other wolves. Bite marks and bruises covered his body and each cheery sound was a knife twisting deeper into his wounds. The other wolves kept silent, licking their egos. The bead loss stung, but worse, far worse, was Tully's face when she pranced the treasures away. She had accused them of offensive remarks, muzzled them, gloved them, and now had stolen something they thought was rightfully theirs. And Maximus, the faithful leader famed for his principles and integrity, the one citizen they thought they should trust, had championed the theft. The wolves were demoralized and clueless as to where to turn.

"I can't take it anymore," roared a young wolf named Greyside. She jumped to her feet. She was brown with a long grey streak along her ribs; young and brash, she was easily agitated. "We need to get our beads back. I don't care if Maximus is a good leader. He had no right to give away what was ours."

Everyone was quiet. Halfear lifted his weary head and grumbled in his gravelly rasp, "The young one has a point."

"Plus," added Greyside, stirred by a spurt of fear, "what if this is part of the sheep's plan? What if Maximus has been in on their scheme the whole time? I never suspected a bear would do what I saw today. It makes no sense."

There was silence again. Wind whistled through the trees. Cheers and laughter echoed from Sheep Pasture. They could almost see their smiles and feel their hooves, those grimy thieving hooves, trying to hold their beads.

Darkfang stood up in the clearing. "I say Maximus returns our beads, and if he refuses"—a maniacal sneer flickered on his face—"there are other, more effective ways to handle these matters."

Another young wolf piped up. "Maybe Maximus had good reason to give away our beads."

"There is no good reason to give away what is ours," barked Ironpaw. He stepped directly into the moonlight cutting through the clearing. Barren fur patches and deep lacerations streaked his face. "Maximus was a good bear, but he has been slipping. In the spring and summer, ever since we found the beads or since that sheep was attacked, something has been off. He rarely leaves that cave. When is the last time you saw him leave other than today? Three months ago? Four? Something is going on, maybe something in his head, maybe something else…" Ironpaw stepped out of the clearing toward the hill. "If you want to do something about this, follow me."

The seven wolves stepped out of the forest and trekked behind Ironpaw through the fence hole and up the hill. Maximus's cave was a short walk in the dark night. Ironpaw lowered his head against the squall that beat around the hill. His face burned against the wind, but his jealousy burned hotter. Tully's words "always second" rung in his ears, and in that moment rage consumed him, rage towards Maximus, rage towards sheep, rage towards everyone. Why had the grizzly betrayed them? Why were the sheep so determined to control the land? Was anyone going to stop this madness? A clod of dirt blew up and splattered Ironpaw's face. He tasted grit through his muzzle and felt the granules scrape his wounds, and he marched harder up the hill.

Without a knock Ironpaw entered the cave. The wolves followed. It was dark inside, lit only by faint moonlight streaming in through the cave mouth. Maximus sat in the room with wide eyes, ready, it appeared, for visitors. "Ironpaw," he said in a sharp tone, somewhat surprised, "Halfear, Darkfang, everyone else, welcome. I wasn't expecting you."

"Forget your courtesy," growled Darkfang. "Why did you give away our beads?"

Ironpaw paced from one wall to the other, tail erect, crouched low, growling beneath his muzzle. "There was no good reason for it, Maximus."

The grizzly stood and raised his chin to get a better look in the darkness. "Was there anyone behind you? I'm expecting someone."

"No," sputtered Ironpaw, frustrated by the bear's distraction. He thought to ask who he was expecting but was too angry about the beads to risk changing the subject. "Answer Darkfang's question: Why did you take our beads?"

Maximus glanced past them out of the cave and was so focused on what might be out there that he hardly seemed to notice the angry wolves. "You're certain you saw no one behind you?"

"There is no one out there," snapped Darkfang. Hardly a muscle moved on his face. "Answer the question."

Maximus drew back his gaze, though by his detached tone it appeared his mind was still elsewhere. "I gave them away to avoid chaos. There was no sense in fighting over stupid beads."

"Is that the real reason?" demanded Ironpaw. He crouched even closer to the ground. "Did someone put you up to this? I know about their plan, Maximus. Did the sheep make you do this? Are you on their side?"

Maximus chuckled, peripherals focused on the seven wolves. It was difficult in the darkness, but he could see their faces, cold and stern, without an ounce of mirth in the bunch. The ones on the edges appeared to inch closer. He thought he imagined it at first, but they shuffled their paws a few inches every few seconds, slowly forming a circle.

"Why do you laugh? You think this is a joke?"

"Sometimes I think this is all a grand joke," said Maximus soberly. "But that is a conversation for other places and other times. I laugh because you think sheep could bribe me. With what: their wool, a portion of those worthless beads? Or do you suggest they threatened me, and I bowed to sheep intimidation?"

"Watch your words. Bah-bahs are more dangerous than you think. They will betray you when they no longer need you."

"No one put me up to this. It was my personal decision."

"Then you're a thief."

Maximus leaped into the moonlight and slammed his monstrous paws against the stone floor. The wolves scampered back, and two fell whimpering on their backs. He was a head higher and four times the size of any of them. "Question my actions if you wish, wolf leader. But never attack my character."

"You stole from your citizens," barked Ironpaw, backing down from the bear.

"I hold loyalties to no citizen. I am loyal to the peace and prosperity of Zoon Garden."

"Then that's it? You'll let the sheep keep our beads?"

Maximus watched them, his nostrils flaring in the cold night air. He said nothing.

"So be it. You live and die by your decisions, Zoon leader." Ironpaw took a quick glance around the cave as though trying to memorize something. Then he lifted his leg, and while he stared into the bear's eyes, he urinated on the cave floor and then the walls. Then Darkfang and Greyside did the same until the cave was rank with the smell of urine. The eight walked out of the cave into the fall night.

12

MAXIMUS WOKE THE next morning frustrated over the night's ordeal. He remained the single citizen immune to the oddities consuming the land and wondered how his citizens had so easily abandoned everything they had once claimed to stand for. Did they fail to realize they no longer stood for it? Had they never stood for it at all? What had happened to the citizens of character with the decrees of life written on their hearts?

Zoon looked nothing like the land he had intended to create. Dwindled was the freedom. Weak was the integrity. Dying were the principles of trust and respect he had founded the land upon. Trapped in thought, clueless what to do, he walked out of his cave to the ledge overlooking the land. There had been a day when he knew what a leader should do. One option was good; one was bad. But good options had run dry. Any decision infuriated someone, and the opposite decision infuriated some-one else. He did not know who was right: him, her, them, no one? The place was utter confusion, and each day it grew more difficult to believe what he saw would resolve itself. Much had already occurred, and a few more days, a few more events, maybe even a few more hours—who knew what odd or irreparable thing could happen next—might set the land on an irreversible course.

A difficult idea plagued Maximus's conscience. He had failed to solve the conundrum or even fully conceptualize it but had come to believe there was much more to know than what Eagle and Owl announced or what Ironpaw and Tully believed. The citizens saw the iceberg's tip and had forgotten to search below the water. The insult, the attack, the chest—it couldn't all be random. It mustn't be; something must be causing it, and everything, Maximus thought, revolved around the office.

In the old days the gray stone building had looked welcoming, but in recent months an eerie aura emanated from its walls. The place looked dark and felt malignant, and though the citizens had long believed in the zookeeper's benevolence, Maximus began to question the nature of the man. He could not comprehend why the zookeeper, whoever he was, had brought such different animals from who knows where to live in the same zoo. The man had to know it would never go well. But he had brought them there anyhow, given them freedom and set them up for failure, Maximus felt, like an experiment for the comical whims of a madman. Why had everyone forgotten about the man who ruled the zoo? Why did no one care that the zookeeper had never been seen?

From his ledge Maximus looked across the road at the office. The gray stone building looked the same: wrought-iron barred windows, three smokeless chimneys, no whisper of Chimp or any movement of life. And then suddenly Maximus saw a dim light flicker on in the third floor window.

"Chimp!" he cried. "Zookeeper! Whoever you are, I see you. Stay right where you are." Maximus leaped off the ledge and galloped down the hillside. But before he took twenty steps, Tweed ran up the hill toward him. Maximus slid to a stop and stared with disgust at the fat panda bear racing to get his attention.

Tweed waved his paw. "Maximus, Maximus, are you headed some place? I need to speak with you. Urgent matters, very urgent, citizens' wishes; can't wait a minute longer."

Maximus glanced past Tweed at the lit window. The light flickered, and he saw a shadow flash across the wall. "What urgent matters? I have no time."

Tweed stopped ten feet short of the grizzly. "You seem on edge, sir. Are you okay?"

"Perfectly well." He looked at the window again. The shadow was moving around the room. He almost yelled out Chimp's name but restrained. "What do you want, Tweed? Spit it out."

Tweed leaned on his heels as if he may run at any moment. "I can tell you later if—"

"Spit it out!"

"There is no easy way to say it!" He cowered and scrunched his ears to his shoulders.

"Say it now, Tweed. I don't have time for your games."

"We desire new leadership! There, I said it. The citizens want new leadership."

Maximus blinked rapidly. His heart rate rose, and blood

rushed to his head. Tweed went on. "Zoon's current condition is not what anyone envisioned or expected. On the Day of Freedom you promised a land of peace, liberty, and justice where citizens would be equal. But today the land is—well, it's not good, Maximus, not good at all. Zoon has done nothing but plummet during your tenure. Some citizens feel oppressed. After yesterday other citizens feel betrayed. They are scared and angry and uncertain about the future."

Blood pounded behind Maximus's eyes. He felt his vision glazing over and animalistic instincts seizing his mind. "I never wanted this. I made the decrees because you said the citizens wanted them. I gave the sheep beads because you told me it would avoid conflict. I have done the citizens' wishes. This is the land they want."

"Shame on you, Maximus, blaming the citizens and I. Should you be honest with yourself, you will see responsibility falls on your shoulders. You are Zoon's greatest problem."

Behind Tweed the light went out. The office looked cold and dark, and the figure was gone. Maximus felt his lips curl beneath his muzzle and saliva pool in his mouth. He tried to blink it away, but he saw bloodlust in his cornea, and then the world turned scarlet. The grizzly reared on his hind legs and slammed his paws into Tweed's chest. The sack of flesh hit the ground in a heap of dust. He curled into the fetal position, squealing, trying to squirm away from the crazed bear. But Maximus pinned Tweed's head to the ground. He ripped off his muzzle and roared at the worthless weeping panda pleading for mercy. Spittle splattered his face, and Tweed smelled the wet stale stench of approaching death.

The roar echoed down the road, through the habitats and into the citizens' ears. Maximus ground Tweed's head into the dirt and sprinted down the hill. "What are you doing?" Tweed shrieked after the charging bear. But no response came and the grizzly launched out of the habitat onto the road.

Dirt covering his face, Tweed frantically waved his paws to the sky. "Owl, Eagle, Pigeon, somebody come here!"

Eagle and Owl swooped down to the hillside. "What happened?" asked Owl. "Why ar—"

"Maximus!" Tweed squealed, flailing his paws. "The bear has lost his mind. Spread the word: a deranged grizzly is on the loose, and will not, I repeat, will not, listen to reason!"

"I'll tell them," said Eagle.

"No, let me do it," said Owl.

"A savage bear is on the loose!" shrieked Tweed. "Both of you tell them. And the pigeons too!"

In a flash the entire tower emptied, and Zoon's sky turned gray with birds. Ordered to execute emergency protocol, the pigeons flew to the ear of any citizen on earth, water, or sky monotonously stating, "Emergency. Loosed bear. Dangerous. Find safety."

With fumbling paws and jittery eyes, citizens bolted locks and stacked rocks behind habitat entrances. Tripping over each other, they poured into caves, up trees, down holes, anywhere they could run to find safety. Then they waited for a sound, a snapped twig, a fallen leaf, a drip of water, or a mammal's scream of agony.

Hearing the vicious roar, Chimp ran downstairs and locked the office's last deadbolt as the enraged bear slammed his mighty paw against the door.

"Where is the zookeeper?" boomed Maximus.

"Maximus, you're in a disoriented state of mind. Consider returning later. Then you can speak with the zookeeper when you are in a clear state of mind."

"I'm in a fully healthy state of mind. Where is he? Open this door!"

"He has departed."

"Departed to where? There is nowhere to go. You lie to me, Chimp." A thunderous paw pounded the door, creaking old hinges and dropping ceiling dust onto the horrified chimpanzee. "I know you hide him in there. Surrender that conniving man so he can answer my questions."

Chimp stood on a chair and peered through the peephole. "He is elsewhere, Maximus. I swear to you he's gone."

Maximus stood on his hind legs and slammed both paws onto the door. "Don't lie to me. If you won't give me the man, then give me yourself."

"I can't do that. You can speak to the zookeeper another day."

Dissatisfied, Maximus stepped back five yards and braced his paws against the asphalt.

"Oh no, please no," whimpered Chimp. He dove off the chair into a pile of cardboard boxes, as seven hundred pounds of muscular flesh rammed the thick office door. Hinges groaned. Steel bent inward. But the door held fast. Maximus stepped back ten yards for another charge. Chimp scrambled to his feet and scurried over boxes and desks and chairs, flinging papers in the air, desperately trying to reach the back staircase.

The grizzly's shoulder hammered into the door. Ceiling lights rattled. Old plaster walls cracked. Maximus ran again and again and again, hurling his full weight into the barricade. The door bent inward with each blow. Air seeped through a gap in the floor. But the resilient bolts held. He gouged deep cuts into the surface and crunched the knob to an indistinguishable shard. Still the door held fast, dented and mangled on its hinges.

Convinced the zookeeper stood inside, Maximus paced around the office, questioning the man's intentions. "I know you watch us. I know you have a plan. What are your reasons? Is it all a show for your entertainment? Will you laugh or cry when it's finished?"

Maximus peeked through the first floor windows and stood to see into the upper rooms. But the windows were dark, and the office remained silent. "Open the door, coward. Tell me your secrets."

Maximus walked around the office until the sun dipped below the western outer wall. The vehement bear at last conceded to the belief that the zookeeper may be elsewhere. Nonetheless, he refused to risk the crafty man slithering back to the office unnoticed the next morning, only to leave unnoticed once more. Maximus cyclically paced around the building. But it was a long siege to wage fueled on emotional rage. A few hours from dawn, in the heart of night, his determination waned. He wanted to stay, but his mind was fuzzy, his eyelids drooped, and his head nodded where he stood. He decided to wait for morning. A fresh mind would do him good, he thought, but not a minute longer, the man and his chimpanzee had avoided his questions for too long, and it was time he knew why.

He walked back across the road toward his hill. In the darkness wolves and sheep watched him trudge up to his cave, none
moving, none speaking, none daring to reveal they had seen
Maximus's weakest hour.

Exhausted, the grizzly pulled his body over the ledge and
crawled into the cave. He curled against the wall and laid his
chin on his arm. Questions for the morning's conversation
reeled in his mind, and his heavy eyelids slammed shut. The
grizzly leader, at rest in his cave after the strenuous ordeal,
breathed heavily, then softly, then slowly.

13

A YOUNG PIGEON three weeks on the job flitted frantically through the sky toward the tower. Her tiny wings beat again and again and pulsed her body through the air. She bulleted through the tower's eastern porthole and, heaving for oxygen, crashed onto the floor.

"Maximus is dead!" The tiny bird swelled for breath. Flustered pigeons leaped down from their coops and surrounded the bird splayed on the ground. "He's dead," she croaked. "Maximus is dead."

The lead pigeon hopped off her roost and shooed the onlookers away. "Move, move, give the poor animal space. Someone bring water." Three pigeons quickly slid over a bowl. The lead pigeon dipped the bird's beak into the cool liquid. She drank deep and sat up, still wheezing and frantic, her green eyes bulging in their sockets. "He's dead. I saw the body. Maximus is dead."

"It's ok. It's ok," said the lead pigeon. She gave the bird another sip of water. "Go slow. Tell us what you saw."

The bird's bulging eyes softened as its breathing slackened. "I flew past the hill ten minutes ago. Maximus was inside the cave. When I looked closer he wasn't breathing…The body has already begun to smell."

"Did you see how it happened? Were any animals nearby?"

"No. I didn't see anything or anyone."

"You did well." The lead pigeon pushed the water closer to the bird. "Please, drink, you have had an exhausting morning." She turned to the hundreds of pigeons perched on roosts already primping wings and clearing throats. "You heard the bird. Make it known: Zoon's leader is dead."

When Tweed and Chimp arrived on scene an hour later, pigeons were still shooting through the air, chirping about the shocking death. Eagle and Owl flew on and off the hill every three minutes asking for updates. Animals had gathered near the hill's base, and they talked of how it had come and what it would mean.

Tweed roped off the cave entrance and ordered no one enter under any circumstance. The stench was tolerable, as he and Chimp knelt beside the body. "Before we begin," said Chimp, his hand hovering over the ears, "the vital question: Was this natural? Or was there foul play?"

Tweed held a sharpened pencil over a fresh parchment roll. "There is always foul play in important matters. Zoon's leader, a bit past his prime, yes, but perfectly healthy—I think few doubt foul play is present; even I can smell it, but prove it? That is another challenge entirely."

"My thoughts exactly." Chimp felt along the throat and over the scalp. He squeezed the ears then the jaw.

Tweed drew his pencil away from the paper. "Before we go further, I must ask: Why have you come out of hiding to inspect Maximus's body?"

"I haven't been hiding."

"No one has seen you since the Day of Freedom. You're a recluse. No, it's worse; you're a ghost. I thought you were either missing or dead."

"The office keeps me busy—many things to do. You know how life can be. This, however, is the most notorious event in Zoon's history. It deserves every second of my time."

"Of course."

"You doubt me?"

"Never. Tell me—where was the zookeeper between the hours of midnight and six?"

Chimp felt inside the body's nostrils and along the gum line. "I thought you might accuse the zookeeper. It does make sense in certain ways."

"Who else could it be but the zookeeper? He witnessed the savage bear pounding at his door and thought he would sleep better without fearing for his life. The bear threatened him. He eliminated the threat."

"It is the obvious explanation, but it could never be the zookeeper. I witnessed the man arrive in the office fifteen minutes after Maximus left, and he stayed in the office well into the morning. If he was in the office when the bear died, he cannot be the murderer."

"You're telling me, the man was missing the whole day while Maximus attacked the office, arrived right when he left, then stayed there until after he died? And I presume you'll tell me, if

I were to walk down this hill right now to the office, he has left again?"

Chimp stroked up the corpse's snout and lifted the eyelids. "It sounds farfetched, I admit. But yes, it is exactly as you say. I can assure you the zookeeper played no role in this." He touched the back of the head near the brain stem. "Ah, here we are. Note: slight indentation at the base of the skull."

Tweed jotted down the observation, and when Chimp looked away, he quickly jotted another small note at the bottom of the page out of his sight. He continued, "If not the zookeeper, then the—"

"Wait one second, I have a question." Chimp paused with his fingers on the corpse's eyelids. "Where were you during all of this?"

Tweed hesitated, evidently peeved by the question. He analyzed the ape and then suddenly lost his temper. "What game are you playing? Are you accusing me? You think I had something to do with this?" Tweed jumped up and looked like he might strike Chimp across the face.

The abrupt rage startled the ape. He leaned away and quickly sputtered a recourse. "No, no , never, nothing of the sort. I simply wanted to know where you were."

"I was in my habitat, hiding for my life like everyone else."

"I see." The ape returned his hands to the corpse's shoulders. "Continue on, as you were saying."

Tweed settled down and brought the pencil back to the parchment but not without giving the chimpanzee another cold stare. "I was saying, if not the zookeeper, then the question turns to who else has motivation for an attack of this nature, and the answer, as you well know, is anyone. What Maximus did, though his intentions were never pinpointed, terrified the animals. His actions had already angered sheep, wolves, cheetahs, giraffes; the entire land was frustrated. They said he was old-fashioned and outdated—a bear who had 'lost his touch.' His rampage of terror made matters worse. My sources tell me animals stayed awake fearful for their lives well into morning."

"Not to mention the odd things he yelled," Chimp interjected. "Did you hear them? The words he shouted to the zookeeper, something about the man's 'reasons,' his 'secrets,' a 'show for his entertainment' and something else about laughter or crying at the end. It was very strange, and sounded, well, it sounded insane to tell you the truth."

"What is your point?"

"Well maybe the animals heard him, and they too thought he was insane and therefore a threat."

"It's possible. Regardless, insanity or not, the point is while I can't say I expected someone to murder him, I wouldn't be surprised if someone did. A frightened animal, or a group of them, might have gained a spurt of courage and carried out this deadly deed."

Chimp was working his way back toward the stomach. His long fingers groped through the matted hair, feeling for bumps or cuts. "I agree, and, from what I can tell, the autopsy shows it could have been anyone. The air smells like viper venom. I haven't found bite marks, but they would be tiny, almost impossible to find beneath this bushy fir. These faint scratches on his snout and those scuffmarks on the ground—you see them there

to the right—could be the result of a struggle. The head indentation is minuscule but clear and perhaps deadly, could be a hoof
stomp, a rock strike, maybe even a kangaroo punch, although
less likely."

"It certainly could. And you know as well as I, half the animals have hard hooves. Also, the food—knowing Maximus's
typical appetite I would deduce he ate a hardy meal after last
night's tirade."

"Edible poison."

"Correct. Anyone could have snuck into the cave and laced
his food. And it wouldn't have to be snake venom. Three plants
across the garden are capable for the job: hemlock, nightshade,
and wolfsbane."

"Let us also remember the chameleons. They hold the power
to enter the cave undetected, a skill any murderer would covet."

Tweed jotted down the observations. "Chameleons, kangaroos, snakes, hooved animals, any animal that can strike with a
rock, any animal that can lace poison, and there may or may not
have been a struggle before death."

Chimp felt the tail and along the legs until he reached the
cold, dead paws. He stepped away from the body and clasped
his hands. "Consider all animals suspects until proven innocent.
I wish you the best of luck in this investigation." The ape walked
out of the cave toward the office. Tweed opened his mouth to
yell a remark, but he suddenly snapped his jaw shut and with
inquisitive eyes peered after ape until he opened the office door
and disappeared inside.

Two days later, in a spurt of solidarity, animals of all species
collected flowers and carried Maximus's body to an aspen grove

near his favorite lake. It was quaint and quiet there, the way he would have liked. They placed him in a deep hole and shoveled dirt over the bear until the brown of his fur was one with the brown of the earth.

The leaders waited eagerly for evidence to come forward. It was assumed someone knew something; someone had heard a conversation or seen an animal sneak into the cave. But a week passed and no one brought forward testimony, not a single peep about the infamous night or the days preceding the tragedy. It appeared citizens were focused on far more pressing matters, chiefly, the protection of their lives.

Raka walked along the cheetah's northern border beside his brother, sniffing and scanning neighboring habitats for threats. Many species had barricaded the fence lines with branches and mud, and scared animals had their heads on swivels. "I'll admit it, Jonesy. I am worried," said Raka. "I don't care if I sound like a coward. No one has seen killing like this. I understand sharp teeth can end an animal's life, but I never thought we would see what, by all angles, is hard, cold, calculated murder."

Jonesy took a large sniff of a bush growing between cheetah and zebra habitats and watched five of the striped horses graze in the field fifty yards away. "I don't blame you. I'm scared too. Any murder is bad but this is even worse. They killed the mightiest animal in Zoon, the animal no one dared challenge."

"If Maximus wasn't safe, no one is safe."

"Exactly. If they killed Maximus, they can kill anyone. And who's to say they won't kill again? Who's to say they won't kill us?" Jonesy stared with suspicion at the zebras, who had begun to whisper and cast glances. "You think it could be one of them?"

"The zebras? Murderers? I doubt it, but maybe. It could be any—" Raka suddenly jumped and spun around.

"What? What is it?" Jonesy lowered his head to the ground and bore his fangs, his tail flicking above his head. "What did you see?"

Raka crouched. His eyes darted left to right and back to left. "I heard something."

"Where? What is it?"

The cheetahs' slender legs tensed. They peered into the tall, dry grass rustling in the wind. After a moment Raka stood upright. "It's nothing. I must have imagined it."

"Goodness, brother." Jonesy heaved a sigh of relief. "You gave me a fright. I was about to run for my life."

"I'm sorry, Jonesy. I've been jumping at noises and walking like someone is behind me. I haven't had a wink of good sleep in three days."

"Neither have I. It's tough to keep my eyes closed, always feel like someone is sneaking up on me." Jonesy went back to watching the zebras. They had stopped grazing altogether and apprehensively watched the cheetahs. Their thigh muscles tensed. They too looked frightened and ready to run. "What was it you were saying?"

"What was it…I…oh, right, I was saying the murderer could be anyone. Giraffes accuse the snakes. Buffalos swear chameleons were involved. Kangaroos say ostriches; armadillos say monkeys. That's the scariest part. No one knows. It could be anyone, Jonesy. It could be you."

"Me? I never murdered him."

"I know, but it's the idea. Bird, mammal, or reptile…stranger, family, or friend—anyone can kill. And any one of us could be the next victim."

By the end of the week the murderer was still at large. The uncertainty terrified the animals. Mortals who lived by law and claw lacked power against an apparent apparition. But the gravest dilemma, perhaps more destructive than the murderer's ambiguity: the dead bear, the venerable founding father, was the emblem of goodness in the land. On that infamous night the stalwart of honor, trust, justice, and animal freedom died.

Despite Maximus's "lost touch," as Tweed tried to claim, most animals had still loved the grizzly. In the shifting sands they had known a leader of character and integrity, the one who championed Zoon's foundational pillars, had lived in the cave at the peak of the hill. With him in place the ship at rough sea had an anchor. They had taken him for granted and never considered a world without Maximus the grizzly. They had never really believed he could die or that one of their own could kill him or that collectively they could drive him to his death. The emblem had been thought immortal, and yet somehow he was buried in a grave by the lake.

Without him there was great uncertainty over the future. The animals sensed a stout leak had sprung in the ship's hull. They felt cold water rising up their legs and the stern tipping toward the deep, and no one knew who or what would stop it.

14

IT WAS THE middle of October at the start of the second week after the death. The young wolf Greyside ran through her habitat, into homes and through the forest, rounding up the pack. "Assemble in the amphitheater! Urgent meeting about the murder. Ironpaw's orders!"

The pack ceased their activities and funneled toward the small, stone amphitheater in the center of Wolf Habitat. Elders took the front seats, adults the middle, and the youths, who had sneaked in, filled the top rows. There was talk of who and what and why, and when everyone had taken a seat, Ironpaw, looking immeasurably irate, walked out of a tunnel into the forum's center. Icy breath puffed through his grass muzzle. Then in one swift motion he ripped off the muzzle and hurled it to the ground. "I won't be silenced!" He tore off his gloves and slammed his silver paw on the stone. "I will not be chained!" The assembly leaped to their feet and ripped off their muzzles and gloves and howled to the sky. They wiggled their freed jaws, stretched their unfettered paws and thought of revenge.

Ironpaw's black nose sniffed the dry air. "Good; yes, that feels good. I won't follow these sheep's illegal decrees. We are free wolves, no matter what the bah-bahs say."

He let them settle and addressed them in a stern tone laden with frustration. "My brothers and sisters, you know why I have called you here. You have seen the atrocities. You have lived them. Our voices silenced, our claws gloved, beads stolen in plain sight, and now, our leader mysteriously murdered—this is no coincidence, my friends. The sheep are on a warpath disguised as a peace march. If there was any doubt, I'm fully confident now, the bah-bahs plan to conquer Zoon and turn the whole land to their soft, fluffy ways."

He leaned his brown snout closer to the audience. His nostrils flared, and his black pupils dilated in their orange irises, as he roved through the amphitheater. "I was in Maximus's cave the night before he died. He was distracted and appeared ready for an expected visitor. They say they don't know who it was...but I know. He was expecting a group of sheep. They arrived late that night after myself and the other wolves had left. They said they came to thank him for the beads, but their true motive was to inspect the cave so they could return the next night and murder him. I warned him; I told him the bah-bahs were more dangerous than he thought, and they would throw him away when they no longer needed him. The next night when darkness fell, Tully and her sheep returned to the cave. She slipped hemlock, an untraceable poison that grows in their pasture, into Maximus's food. He returned late in the night, ate his food, and the next morning was found dead. The sheep murdered Maximus in cold blood."

There were a great deal of gasps as nearly everyone was shocked, and the wolves began to glance around and whisper. "The sheep look nice; they appear innocent, but beneath those kind faces they're more ruthless than we could ever imagine. Hear me, my brethren, the days of peace and good intentions are behind us. As we speak the sheep further their plan. They say we are equals; they say Zoon Garden is the land of all animals, but they want Zoon Garden to be the land of the sheep." The wolf tried to keep calm, but his voice quivered with rage. Lips curled, yellow stained fangs bared, he circled the amphitheater. "Defeat is not a swift strike; it is subtle disintegration. It moves slow, coiling its way around the feet, the stomach, the chest... by the time you feel its pressure, it already has your throat. These sheep and their supporters intend to crush our way of life. Every one of you, mark my words, if we do nothing, soon the bah-bahs will rule Zoon."

Ironpaw's lips wrapped back around his fangs. He bowed his head and stepped aside, a signal to open the assembly for remarks. The stoic wolves sat still, muscles tense and minds churning. Then Darkfang stood. His long, black tail swung like a whip, and his voice froze the air. "I swear an oath to you all: while I breathe a bah-bah will never rule Zoon. They'll have to step over my cold, dead corpse to get to the cave."

"Aye! Down with the bah-bahs."

"We won't let them destroy Zoon!"

Ironpaw smiled and watched the wolves cheer. "Well said, Darkfang. They'll have to kill us all before a sheep controls our land. We will crush them and end this chaos the sheep created."

The assembly erupted with applause. The wolves jumped

and howled, yearning for revenge. Amidst the cheers, Ironpaw leaped atop a rock and repeatedly slammed his paw onto the stone. "This morning Tweed appointed us lead investigators. He plans to create new decrees to help us catch the murderer. We will expose this scheme to the animals and convict the sheep of their crimes. We will restore the true Zoon. We will save Zoon Garden."

About this time, on the hill's eastern side, Tully ordered her flock into the valley for an urgent announcement. The sheep populace, now approaching one hundred and fifty, huddled shoulder to shoulder in the cold, waiting for their leader to speak. Out of fear they had taken to walking everywhere in groups of ten and yearned to be comforted.

Tully walked out onto her knoll. Her crisp white wool was long and faded, dirtier than it had been. She looked disturbed, as though worry had riddled her mind since the murder. The cynical observer might have also conceded a hint of fear hid in her eyes. But her zeal was strong, and the flock heard the urgency in her voice. "I must be frank," she said, "it's a dangerous time to be sheep. A murderer is on the loose. Tweed tells us the investigation is underway and the killer is unknown. I wish it were true. It would be less dangerous for our kind if the murderer were unknown. But the truth—oh, I wish it were not true…" She choked up and a tear spilled down her snout. "The truth is the wolves murdered Maximus."

"No!" cried Snowy, almost bursting into tears. "Don't tell us that."

"I wish it was false, but I know for certain Ironpaw and his wolves murdered Maximus. The day our bear leader gave us our beads Ironpaw had murder on his heart; you remember, he told me he would kill me. Those selfish monsters were angry, and that night they demanded Maximus return our beads, but Maximus refused. This enraged Ironpaw, and the next night, when Maximus was tired from circling the office, the wolves returned to the cave. They ambushed him in the darkness. He fought them off, biting them and clawing them—look at the wolves' faces; they have bruises and cuts, and if you ask they won't tell you how they got them. The bear fought valiantly, but he was weak from the day and there were too many wolves. Once they subdued him they held him down and dropped a rock on the base of his skull to frame another species. The wolves murdered Maximus in cold blood."

There was a brief silence. "But that means the murderers hate us," said Snowy, her voice trembling.

"Yes. The murderers are our enemies, and they hate us. This has been part of the wolves' plan since the beginning. Ironpaw bided his time until he could eliminate Maximus and conquer the land in the name of the wolves. With Maximus gone Ironpaw lacks physical opposition. He'll take back our beads, oppress weaker animals, and destroy all we have accomplished. He'll try to dominate us, likely with violence. If he has killed once, he will do it again. Stay together. Don't let your friends or family out of sig—"

"Why is this happening?" a young lamb cried. He began to sob in the front row.

"Why are wolves so cruel?" whimpered another.

"We don't deserve this."

"We didn't do anything wrong."

Tully walked down into the flock and nuzzled against the whimpering sheep. "I know. It's not your fault. It's those vicious wolves. They're terrible, terrible animals, selfish and mean and violent. But we can't let these brutes intimidate us. You are sheep; you are strong. If there was a time to resist, it's now. We will weather the winds of oppression and fight back against the wolves. We will save Zoon Garden."

Sheep spirits started to lift, but suddenly Eagle jetted overhead. Transfixed by sunlight, her magnified shadow darkened half the pasture. She unleashed a violent screech the sheep could only imagine was the cry an eagle made before it slayed prey. They ducked, expecting an attack, and lambs hid beneath their mothers. But the white-crested bird soared past. She landed on the hill's tallest tree and with lungs full of bitter wintry air announced, "Attention, animals, due to our land's turbulent times Tweed has ratified Zoon's Third Decree: In times of great trial, a new decree may be enacted without leader markings." Cold air hissed around the golden-beaked bird as she waited for the words to sink in. After a moment she continued, "To restore safety we must capture the murderer roaming our land. By the power of the Third Decree, I announce the Fourth Decree of Zoon Garden: In times of great trial, wolves may enter any habitat to confiscate citizens' pertinent and suspicious materials."

Eagle launched back into the cold air. She had not flown but fifty feet when Owl suddenly broke through a cloud. He plummeted two hundred feet, wings tight to his body, beak guiding the wind past. He flattened out and entered straight into a tirade. "Unapproved! These decrees are unapproved! Animals don't want wolves to search our habitats. This is a violation of our rights. It's an illegal act, illegal!"

Eagle flew below him and screeched louder. "Ignore this foolish chicken. The land is in a chaotic time. We must have the power to restore peace."

"She's lying to you," Owl shrieked, dropping lower. "The wolves want to seize control. They will steal our rights and throw us back in cages." The two birds continued to squabble and scream well into the night.

At dusk the same day, near the time when the sun and moon fight to rule the sky, Ironpaw stood at the head of twenty wolves, two lines of ten, a younger wolf paired with an older, and waited for the sun to set. "Tonight the bah-bahs' luck runs dry," he snarled, watching the sun descend. A spit of foam hung on the edges of his mouth, and his eyes were wide and crazed. "No matter how well they covered their tracks, we will tear through this land and bring the sheep to justice."

When the full moon had risen high enough to illuminate the road, the pack moaned a gory, ghastly howl and pounded onto the cold asphalt. Frustrated by their lack of discipline, Ironpaw had mandated a new training regiment: organized marching. The pack's legs stepped in unison, front legs lifting high in the air, tails swinging in beat to Darkfang's cadence. At two hundred yards Ironpaw pointed his long-clawed silver paw at the koala's door. The duo at the rear broke off and pounded on the steel door. "Open up! We're here to inspect." Feet shuffled and there were sounds of resistance, but the door swung open and the pair swept inside.

It continued that way, rear guard forking off left and right into the habitats at Ironpaw's command. Sometimes the animals opened. Sometimes the wolves broke down the barrier. Under full moon's light, they tore through the fields and meadows. They combed the grass for poison and stuck their snouts into anything they deemed suspicious. They raided every cave and scrutinized every acre. And to any who protested, they snarled and snapped their unmuzzled jaws.

All night howls rang through the land as wolves shoved animals aside and carried bags of seized evidence back to Wolf Habitat. Ironpaw circled the six-foot-high pile of rubbish. He shoved his head deep into the mound, looking for sheep wool or bear fur, and did not hear the cries of innocent animals as his wolves ransacked their habitats.

15

ALL EVIDENCE WAS collected and analyzed. Nothing suspicious was discovered, neither clues, nor hints, nor scent of a lead. It had proved a strenuous ordeal to seize nearly every item in Zoon and drag it to Wolf Habitat. Most of the pack was exhausted, asleep in the forest, curled up tight, snouts tucked to their chests. Ironpaw, however, could not justify a wink of rest while the murderer remained at large. He sought Tweed's approval to further the investigation. But no one could find Tweed for two days, and when they finally did, it took him another day to chisel the Fifth Decree's stone. Then he disappeared again, something about "important matters and running out of time."

It was near November when Eagle declared the land's fifth law: In times of great trial, citizens must confess to wolves any information deemed necessary to land's well-being.

Not five seconds after Eagle finished, Ironpaw and a select group with slabs of bark strapped to their backs stomped into the road toward Giraffe Habitat. They marched at a quick pace in the dawn light, and in two minutes Ironpaw knocked on the habitat's entrance. They heard patter of tiptoeing hooves, and Isabella's head popped over the fence. She looked a great deal older than she had, less amiable, and more sullen. Her face was thin and neck hunched, but her mighty prowess remained, as did her pride, and she did not condone wolf harassment. She raised her head as high as it would go and glared at the pack. "Are you here to abuse us or steal more of our possessions?"

A bark gurgled in Ironpaw's throat, but he gritted his teeth and choked it down. "We're here for interviews to find information about the murder."

"You're a disgrace. Your decrees are illegal, and you're tearing this land apart. I have no information to give corrupt animals like you."

"You'll give us whatever information we want," roared Ironpaw. He rammed into the entrance and began chewing on the handle. "Open this door. Open it now. You can't keep me out. I'll break it down."

Isabella ducked her head behind the fence and turned to her herd. Twenty giraffes of different sizes and ages stood near the watering hole. Grim glares plastered their faces, and the young ones wrapped their necks around the elder's legs. "We can't stop them," she said.

"Let them in," said Sharif. "We have nothing to hide. We're not murderers."

"Ok, I will. But before I do, everyone remember: when they interrogate you whatever you say can and will be twisted and used against you."

With her hoof she kicked the lever's handle, and the door swung open. Ironpaw rushed into the habitat and began pulling and pushing giraffes apart. "Break up! We will question you one at a time. If you're truthful, this will be quick and painless. If you lie, we will stay here for days."

The wolves nipped the giraffes' ankles, separating them into groups. They grabbed the prime interviewees, those cursed with dubious eyes, and forced them into isolated areas. Ironpaw grabbed a young giraffe by the tail. He led the half-grown animal to a secluded place along the fence beneath a marula tree. He rested his side against the tree and encouraged the giraffe to lie on a nearby rock if he wished. Once they both had settled, Ironpaw pulled out his slab of bark and laid it on the ground. "Do you know why I selected you?"

The giraffe was small for his age with large, black, unsullied eyes and a round head that looked clumsy on his long neck. He had a childishly high-pitched voice. "Because I was the first you saw?"

"Wrong. It's because young animals are honest. They speak the truth. They don't yet know the games adults play with words and tricks and lies. Will you speak the truth to me?"

"Yes," he answered in a timid, quivering voice.

"Good. I will do the same to you. First, tell me your name."

"Georgie."

"Georgie the Giraffe. No middle name?"

"Correct."

Ironpaw etched a quick note into the bark slab with his claw. "And how many seasons are you?"

"Seven."

"Good. My first question: Where were you the night of Max-imus's murder?"

"In our habitat, hiding with my family."

"Were all the giraffes in the habitat?"

"Yes."

"Were any sheep with you?"

"No."

"Have you spoken to any sheep?"

"I think I did once a long time ago."

"How long ago?"

"I'm not sure."

"Tell me how long ago, Georgie."

"I don't know," he squeaked. "I really don't know. Maybe three seasons."

"Unfortunate." Ironpaw scratched two side annotations in the ledger.

"What do those marks mean?" the young giraffe asked, trying to peek over the bark.

"Don't concern yourself with those. What specifics can you tell me about the night of the murder? Take me through it step by step."

"It was a normal day. Then I heard the warning. A pigeon came and told me to hide. I saw lots of pigeons going to other animals so I knew it was real. My family and I hid from the bear. Then we waited, and I was scared. My sister held me the whole night. Then he never came. I was happy."

"I'm sure you were. Many animals were happy to be alive that next morning. But Maximus was dead. How does that make you feel?"

"Bad. I don't like that an animal died."

"Nor do I. I like it less that we don't know how he died.

Here is my dilemma, Georgie. Maximus was a healthy bear. He kept a clean diet. He maintained his fitness. He was in the middle of his prime. Someone must have killed him. That is the single explanation."

"It wasn't me."

"I know you're innocent. But someone killed him, someone in Zoon, maybe someone you know, maybe one of your friends, maybe that sheep you spoke to three seasons ago." Ironpaw leaned off the tree toward the young giraffe. "I need to know if you know the killer. That's the single reason I have come here, and please, I beg you, for your own sake, tell me the truth."

While the interviews continued in Giraffe Habitat, five minutes east Tully stormed in circles. Hesitant to intervene, Snowy watched her leader fume through the habitat. Her jaw was tight, as if she had ground her teeth in frustration for hours and the slightest provocation would set her off. With an indignant look between tears and rage, she at last turned to her group of loyal advisors. "They won't stop. No matter the lack of evidence, they'll ruin our reputation and make us the murderers."

"Who will, ma'am?" asked one advisor.

"Who? Who! The wolves! Did you not hear them marching down the road? Did you not hear the animals' cries? A pigeon told me as we speak the wolves are ruthlessly interrogating the giraffes. And after them they will interrogate our other allies until someone admits a sheep murdered Maximus. The wolves are determined to convict our species for murder even if they have to coerce animals to make false confessions."

"That's not fair," cried another advisor.

"It's utterly unfair. But wolves have never cared about fairness. These are rights violations, clear as day. They lack evidence, yet know we are guilty. It will never end. Ironpaw will convince Tweed to make another decree and after that, another. He's adamant to find this murderer, convinced it's one of us because he hates us, and will blindly hunt us till we're wrongly convicted.

"And I'll tell you why he's adamant. I'll tell you why he'll push this past the point of clear innocence: he needs a scapegoat. He needs to distract the animals, because if they stop to think for a moment's breath they will realize he's the murderer." She shook her head, as if to wish mercy upon the blind souls that had yet to see the light. "He hides his guilt in front of the animals' eyes. While they argue over who killed the founding father, the murderer himself convinces the land he's a patriot."

"Oh my," gawked Snowy

"Oh my is right!" The sheep leader threw her nose toward the sky. "Owl! Come here! Owl! Come quickly! The animals must know the truth."

The sheep could hear the brown bird's voice somewhere high in the air. "I will say it till I die. These decrees are illegal and these wolves are criminals!" It was hard to see through the clouds, but somewhere near him they heard Eagle screeching, "Praise our wolf brothers for their diligence during this trying time. They will find the murderer and restore peace to our land." Tensions were peaking between the two birds as they became more desperate to prove their points. One hardly spoke without the other immediately shouting louder.

At Tully's beckon Owl's voice suddenly stopped. He glided

down over the sheep's heads and landed in the pasture. His voice was hoarse, and his head twitched with adrenaline. He hadn't slept in days. "What do you want? I have no time. I can't leave her up there alone. The whole land will become ignorant wolf lovers."

"I won't take more than a minute," said Tully. She turned away from the flock and looked Owl in his large eyes. "Ironpaw is out of control."

"I know. He's invading habitats, looting possessions, interrogating innocent animals; the wolf is a maniac."

"He's absolutely psychotic. He hasn't tried to investigate anyone but our friends. And he continues to target weaker animals. He won't stop, Owl. You have to tell the animals the truth before it's too late. You must tell them Ironpaw murdered Maximus."

"He's a crazed lunatic, Tully. If we tell them, he'll murder us too."

"It's a risk we must take. A few more actions, one or two more decrees, and Ironpaw will have complete power. He'll oppress the animals, and we will lack the strength to stop him."

Owl looked up in the sky. He could hear Eagle far away, now yelling about "necessary evils to restore peace."

"I…I must get back," sputtered Owl.

"Tell them, Owl. Tell them quickly before something worse happens."

The barn owl dove off the knoll, disappeared for a second, and then soared upward to the sky's center. Beneath him the animals were engaged in daily activities. Owl watched them sip water and patrol their borders. Then he sucked in the largest breath he could and screeched so loud he thought his vocal cords would tear. "Attention, everyone! The murderer has been found. I repeat, the murderer has been found." The animals' eyes darted skyward like mice with cheese raised above their heads. They watched the brown bird glide side to side in the bright morning light. Nothing moved. Even the trees seemed to hold their breath. "The murderer has lived in the open amongst us. It's obvious, so obvious we nearly missed it. My dear animals, the murderer is the wolf leader Ironpaw!"

Owl watched the animals' faces fill with sudden revelation. Then a brown and white and golden blur flashed in his periphery. Eagle shot through the air and knocked Owl out of the sky. The birds fell fifty feet, pecking and gouging.

"That's a lie!" shrieked Eagle, breaking away from him and flying lower to be heard. "Owl is a liar. The sheep are the true murderers. They plotted Maximus's death since the beginning."

Owl flapped his wings in her face and moved whichever way she tried to fly. "Ignore this fool. The sheep care for the animals."

"No they don't. Sheep are deceptive; don't trust the bah-bahs. They snuck into Maximus's cave and poisoned him with hemlock."

"No! The wolves dropped a rock on his skull. They were always jealous. They wanted to kill him so they could control Zoon."

The two birds sped over the land, yelling the same message, one for the sheep, one for the wolves, but in different voices with different interpretations. Beneath them the animals watched the calamity, unable to break their gazes, and screamed encouragements to their preferred bird.

"Please, everyone," begged Owl. "You must believe me. Ignore Eagle and the wolves. Tully loves this land. Sheep want the true Zoon. Sheep will fix this place and make it a land for all animals."

Eagle flapped harder and flew past him. "The sheep are lying to you. They look kind, but they're deceptive beasts. They want a land where everyone is a sheep. Wolves will restore true Zoon."

Owl dropped to Eagle's elevation and glided parallel. "Quit your ignorant remarks for a moment and let an intelligent bird speak."

"Absolutely not. You're never quiet for me. You're a rude ill-informed bah-bah supporter." Eagle dove down to three hundred feet elevation. "Animals, please, I promise you the sheep are—" She heard a sudden whoosh behind her and turned to see Owl plummeting toward her, razor sharp talons extended. It was too late to flee. She flung her own legs up and caught his talons before they pierced her chest.

Talons locked, neither able to fly, they flapped haphazardly, screeching through the air, neither willing to let go.

"The sheep are murderers!"

"The wolves killed Maximus!"

"I swear upon the hill, it's the sheep!"

"Lies! Ironpaw will destroy the land!"

The animals watched the two birds spin in circles tumbling out of the sky, clawing, pecking, tearing out feathers, pulling each other toward the ground.

16

THE SUN WAS near set. The wolves had sat on the amphitheater's cold stone steps since Owl and Eagle's fight that morning, and until five minutes prior, they had been nowhere close to an agreement. Ironpaw's hackles bristled along his nape, and his tail curled tight above his hindquarters. His voice was gruff like he had been shouting for hours. "I say it again, Halfear, the sheep are shameless, not a particle of honor in their flock. Right as we were getting close, two, three, maybe one interview away, the bah-bahs have the nerve to publicly accuse us, us—the very investigators trying to solve the murder. We were so close; the giraffes were cracking."

Ironpaw walked toward Sheep Pasture, sniffing the ground, jerking his eyes to the sky. "Tully must have known, someone must have told her we were close to the truth. That's why she accused us, to throw us off the trail. And those stupid animals, those imbecile koalas and armadillos, actually believe her. She's deceived them for years, and they still think she's their savior! I don't care if you disagree, Halfear; it's time to attack the sheep."

Halfear sat on his hind, stoic and composed, and watched
the wolves' ears perk at the mention of an attack. He swore he
saw Darkfang smile for the first time, and two of the younger
wolves licked their lips. "Easy, Ironpaw. I'm on your side. I want
to rip their throats out too. But, as I said before, we must avoid
anything drastic. If we attack the sheep, they'll gain the animals'
sympathies. We would look like violent monsters, the very thing
they say we are."

"No, no, you're right. We won't physically attack them, not
yet. This will be a different kind of attack. If the bah-bahs want
to scream and lie to sway the populace, we must shout the truth
louder." Ironpaw looked up in the amphitheater. "Darkfang,
where is Darkfang? There you are; come here."

The large wolf with tar-black fur walked down the rocks. His
stained incisors jutted out beneath his lip, and his untethered
claws flexed against the stones. Ironpaw placed his paw on the
wolf's chest. "I have a task for you: go to the tower and recruit
the loudest pigeons. Work a deal with the pigeon leader where
wolf messages move to the front of the announcement list. Do
you understand?" Darkfang bowed and took off into the dusk
in the direction of Pigeon Tower.

Ironpaw looked at the rest of the pack. "We're going to
make the bah-bahs regret they destroyed our free land. Get
some rest. Be at the highest cliff by dawn. The attack begins at
first light."

From dusk till midnight, Ironpaw divided the pack into three
squadrons: the Tully Defamation Squadron, the Sheep Conviction Squadron, and the Wolf Savior Squadron, squadrons one,
two and three, for short. He knew the animals were desperate.

Scared, clueless, and uncertain of the future, they would listen to anyone who promised them what they wanted to hear. Victory lay in convincing the animals that wolves would quell their worries, wolves would heal their ills, and in the end wolves would save them.

After midnight Darkfang ran back into the habitat. In the darkness he crashed into a thorny bush, but he plowed through it and sprinted onto the highest cliff, his cold breath billowing like fog around him. He found Ironpaw awake at the edge of the precipice, looking past the hill into the sheep's pasture. "Sir, the pigeons have agreed. They'll be here at dawn."

The wolf leader kept his eyes on the pasture. In the faint moonlight he could see the flock nestled together against the wind, Tully in the center, her chest rising and lowering with each breath. "Good. We will have messages ready for them." He motioned for the younger wolf to join him on the cliff ledge. "You know, it's a shame, Darkfang, I never wanted this. I wish those sheep had been more reasonable. I wish they hadn't put their slimy hooves into everyone's business. Why couldn't they keep to their pasture and let us live how we wished?"

The younger wolf opened his mouth to respond, but Ironpaw began again. "We have many long days ahead of us, Darkfang. Go get some rest. We will need you at your best." Darkfang jogged off toward his cave, his smiling fangs shining brightly in the darkness. Ironpaw laid down, one paw over the other, eyes fixated on the pasture.

Faintish purples and tints of red glossed the horizon, slowly dissipating a thick morning fog. Wolves began to arrive on the cliff limbered and eager. Ironpaw split them into their three

squadrons and lined them up on the cliff's ledge. A soft hum of
flapping wings stirred in the distance, and one hundred and fifty
of the tower's loudest pigeons flew through the evaporating fog
onto the cliff. In the past ten months the population had bred
at extraordinary rates. Nests covered the roof and peppered the
structure's timber beams. The tower had literally overflowed
with birds. There were thousands of them, each eager to make
announcements.

Darkfang walked down the battle line. "At ready, prime messages!" The pigeons hopped up to the line, and the wolves whispered instructions in the birds' ears. Darkfang watched the coming dawn. "Birds ready. On my signal." The pigeons unfurled
their wings. "Wait for it. Wait for it,"—sunlight erupted over
the horizon—"Fire!" One hundred and fifty birds catapulted
into the morning sky. They climbed, climbed, climbed, and then
exploded with jabber.

"Tully is dishonest and malicious!"

"Sheep murdered Maximus. They restrict our speech!"

"Wolves bring justice. They will stop the sheep!"

"Ironpaw is innocent! Tully is corrupt."

All morning the wolves fired pigeon volleys and bombarded
the sky with words and arguments and wolf-truth. And it appeared to be working. Reality in the sky had long before become
reality on the ground. Impressionable animals, still fearful for
their lives, searching for meaning, looking for answers, uncertain what to believe, submitted to wolf-truth after four, three,
sometimes only one well-crafted pigeon projectile.

Tully sprinted through the pasture beneath the coos and
whistles of discharging pigeons. "We're under attack! Everyone

get to the knoll!" She head-butted a sheep on the rump. It took off toward the highest part of the pasture, and the rest of the sheep stampeded after it. "Snowy! Snowy!" She shouted at the top of her voice over the deafening birds. "Where are you? Snowy!"

"Here, ma'am, I'm here." The lead advisor wriggled past the stragglers to her superior. She was in a great fright and kept glancing at the screeching pigeons above. "Ma'am, they'll trick the whole land. Everyone is going to become a wolf supporter."

"We will stop them. We must for the animals' sake. Snowy, I'm putting you in charge. Organize the flock. Send pigeons into the sky. I give you full authority." Tully shoved her toward the knoll, but then hooked her hoof and pulled her back. "Snowy, listen to me. This is war. It's no time for kindness. The flock doesn't need a comforter; they need a commander. Set aside your niceness or we will lose and the wolves will conquer Zoon. Do you understand?"

"I understand."

"Promise me."

"I swear it." Snowy took off through the pasture. She muscled her way to the knoll and found sheep confused and bumbling, half of them watching the wolves' pigeons. "You fools! Call down a bird before the wolves take more ground." The frantic sheep waved their hooves at the sky, screaming for pigeons. Within fifteen minutes, Snowy launched her counterassault. Sheep pigeons discharged dogma canisters and popped myopic flares, and sheep-truth lit the sky ablaze.

"Wolves oppress small animals. Wolf hatred destroys our land!"

"Tyrannical wolves will crush us all!"

"Sheep will stop the violence. Sheep are our only chance!"

Screeching pigeons covered the sky east to west as far as the eye could see. The same impressionable animals watched the sheep's birds and found themselves angry at the wolves and empathetic toward the sheep. Thus, the ongoing skirmish exploded into the War on Truth.

17

TELL THEM DARKFANG thrashes any creature that disobeys him," Snowy shouted, sprinting along a sheep battle line. Her hooves tore up the grass, as wolves' pigeons screeched above and sheep waited for her orders. "Fuzzy, I need you to say, 'Wolves discriminate against peacocks.' Marvin, you say, 'Wolves steal our beads.' Tinsy, you tell them Ironpaw bit an armadillo."

"When did he do that, ma'am?"

Snowy had already passed. She turned around, nose scrunched and eyebrows furrowed. She stood over the younger sheep. "What did you say?"

"I asked when did Ironpaw bite an armadillo?"

"When did Iron…" The sheep commander chuckled and bit her lip. A drip of blood dribbled down her chin. "Do you want the wolves to conquer the land?"

"No, ma'am, they would destroy Zoon."

"Then you want to win this war?"

"Yes, I want to win the war."

"Then shut your stupid mouth and announce what I say. That goes for all of you. There will be no disobedience in this army. You'll do as I say and say what I tell you." She ran to the end of the battle line. "Pigeons, ready!" She lifted her hoof and swung it down. "Fire!"

On the hill's opposite side, wolves dashed around pine trees and scrambled onto the cliff. Pigeons sped from cliff to sky and sky to cliff, grabbing messages from the wolves. Their fatigued voices croaked, but they shouted all the louder. Darkfang stood on a boulder in the center barking out orders. "By hour's end I want eighty more birds in the air attacking Tully's integrity. Squadron one, you call the bah-bahs thieving maggots. Squadron three, affirm whatever Eagle says. And someone, anyone, shut up that damn owl."

It was early December, and the War on Truth had been raging for weeks. Some days sentiments surged toward sheep-truth, other days the battle bulged toward wolf-truth. But by and large the war had held to a stalemate. Snowy and Darkfang, however, were discontent with anything but absolute victory. The two creatures had devolved into a special breed of despicable creature. They were ignorant fanatics wholly and singularly committed to their species. They were stubborn in their ways, and unrelenting in their opinions. They believed one side existed to every argument, one side alone, and that one viewpoint somehow, through intellectual flips, spins and acrobatic maneuvers, proved their every belief. They never admitted wrong, never acknowledged the validity of another's idea, and never allowed a tinge of empathy. When necessary they vehemently lied to preserve the illusion of truth. If a counter idea wormed its way into their conscience, and they found themselves, despite every attempt to resist, sympathetic toward some false notion, they would cover their ears, babble nonsense, and flee to where they could reinoculate with their native ideology. If they ever, at any point, or for any reason, began to stray from this criterion, it was their duty to renounce their position. Their tribe would then appoint another, thereby allowing the dogma to live beyond the individual. In this way many successive war leaders could perish, dozens if necessary, erased from memory, but the impenetrable idea, the heartbeat of the tribe, the species' truth, would remain immortal.

It was a difficult task, neither for the sane of mind nor the valiant of heart, but Darkfang and Snowy, zealous beyond comparison, thrived in their roles. In the first week the two sides had deployed traditional tactics: argumentation, logic, compulsion, but as stakes rose and the battle intensified, the war had become no longer about truth; it had become about ideological reality and the attempt to make that reality the truth. Regardless of contrary proofs or sound antithetical arguments, the sheep and the wolves had begun to shout anything they thought might sway a creature. Logic did not matter. Facts did not matter. Truth was neither what had occurred nor failed to occur; truth was whatever the creatures believed. And with enough practice they could make them believe anything. Truth had become a battleground won by the species that shouted loudest.

Insults burst in air. Dogma bombs dropped on creatures' skulls. Slander shrapnel shredded the masses. It was a nasty ordeal, void of physical harm, but full of disparagement and personal assaults deployed to destroy the opposition's integrity and reputation. They were no longer two species with two visions; they were two tribes dwelling in separate realities, yet inhabiting the same single, unalterable reality. Each morning brought a new slur, each evening a new slight. But more than anything, the two tribes continued to insist the land's problems fell squarely and wholly on the other tribe's shoulders.

For the first few days, the tactics had been exceptionally effective. Worried creatures continued to swarm to both tribes' promises, cheering when the leaders told them what they wanted to hear. Huge portions of the population came to believe that wolf-truth or sheep-truth was The Truth. But as the war stretched on and armament increased and demonization triumphed, casualties piled up. Honesty lay dead in a ditch, integrity and respect, beaten and tortured, were buried together in a shallow grave, and reason swung from a noose, purple and bloated, at the top of the hill. The creatures began to realize neither the sheep nor the wolves cared for the land or for them. They cared for victory alone, and they would destroy the land to attain it.

No creature knew what to believe or who to follow, who was telling the truth or who was lying to the masses. Facts had once meant undeniable reality. Opinions had once meant an individual's belief. But in Zoon Garden opinions had become facts; facts had become opinions, and truth, if it still existed, hid somewhere in the muddled morass. The creatures doubted whether what they had been told for seasons was true. They doubted what the birds said. They doubted what Tweed told them. They of course doubted who killed Maximus. Some even doubted whether Maximus had actually died. They had witnessed his breathless nostrils, his stilled heart, his body lain in the ground. But in that season of Zoon Garden, creatures were uncertain they could trust what their eyes saw, or what their ears heard, or even what their own minds believed.

Koalas had begun to sleep twenty-three hours per day with wads of leaves rammed in their ears. The once amiable capybaras stayed isolated and lonely for days at a time. In sporadic bursts of rage, monkeys flung coconuts at other creatures. Raka spent his waking hours infuriated by anything either side said. He rattled the fence and screamed curses and asked how much longer the insanity would continue. Sometimes he ran sprints in frustration; sometimes he screamed at the top of his lungs; rumor had it he sometimes was even seen clawing his own ears and gouging his own eyes. The creatures had nothing to trust, no goal to pursue, nothing to believe, and they seemed to have lost their sanity. But nothing was more telling than Isabella. She slept poorly during the war. Her ears rang and head hurt; she was less blissful, less optimistic, and for the first time in her life she questioned why she continued living.

When the last leaves began to break from their branches and swirl about in the wind, she walked out of her hut to find her mate. Sharif knelt outside near the watering hole. He too looked mellow and solemn with his tail hung low as he gazed at the ground. They knelt near the pool together and watched the pigeon battle reflect off the water's surface. Isabella dipped her tongue and drew a cool sip. "Do you remember—it was many seasons ago—what Maximus said the day he freed the land?"

Sharif closed his eyes. He strained to remember anything

from the earliest days. "I think he said in Zoon Garden we would have life, we would have liberty, and we would be happy."

"Yes that's what I remember. I must tell you, Sharif. I don't feel alive. I don't feel free. I'm not happy."

"Neither am I." He watched the battle above. The bird cloud was so thick it was hard for him to determine whether it was night or day. "Where do you think they went?"

"Who?"

"Life, liberty, happiness."

Isabella titled her neck and watched the chaos in the sky. "I don't know. But I don't blame them for leaving."

They knelt near the water in silence, dreary and tired, and wondered what had gone wrong.

18

THE WAR CONTINUED. The voice of the many remained in the lips of the few. And the power of thousands stayed in the hands of two. There were many tales and signs, and though it had been thought impossible, the wolves and sheep taught the creatures to hate each other more.

The creatures held tight to the captainless ship with shredded sails and broken masts flinging about the sea. They bailed water and plugged holes, but there was an overwhelming sense that the water was too high, the ship was too sunk, and soon they would be forced to abandon that mighty vessel. They pleaded with the sheep and the wolves. But Tully and Ironpaw raised their voices, doubled war efforts, and pressed on toward victory.

On the last day of fall, when the trees were barren and the war was in full force, Tweed appeared on the road in front of the office. No one had seen the black and white bear for weeks. There were rumors he had abandoned the land in the turmoil, but there he stood, somber, slimmer than they recalled, staring at the office's door.

No one noticed him for a few minutes. Then Eagle saw him. And seconds later Owl spotted him. The black and white bear squinted and strained, appearing to ponder a difficult concept. It was a strange sight, almost eerie; he hardly blinked and looked as though he would go on standing in front of that office for eternity.

Distracted by the peculiar sight, both birds stopped screeching. The pigeons too began to quiet. Confused as to why their birds had hushed, the wolves and sheep looked about and saw Tweed standing in the road. For first time in months, the whole land went silent, fascinated by the bear that stood at the office door.

After a minute creatures began to whisper.

"Where has he been?"

"What is he looking for?"

"What does he see?"

The office looked like the once-mighty fortress of a king who had died and whose guards had fled along with all of its eminence. Cobwebs clung to the building's walls, and the mortar joints were crumbling. Grime was now covering its windows, and stones had fallen from its chimneys. The creatures peeked through the fence lines and wondered what Tweed was seeing inside that decaying edifice.

"He's trying to find Chimp," said someone.

"No, he's looking for the zookeeper."

Some ten minutes passed. Unable to endure the tension any longer, Ironpaw walked into the road and stood beside Tweed. Darkfang and the pack followed. Not wanting to be outdone,

Tully tottered cautiously out of her pasture with Snowy and her advisors.

At the sound of hooves clacking asphalt, Ironpaw's ears perked. His mouth salivated and lips curled. "You stupid bah-bahs, you ruined everything." The wolf leader spun around, snapping his jowls. "You destroyed Zoon Garden!"

It was the first time the wolves and sheep had made eye contact since the day Maximus gave away the beads. The pack sprang into a pincer formation. The sheep ran forward and surrounded Tully. She slammed her hooves and tried to push through them. "How dare you blame me, you monster! It's your fault! You destroyed true Zoon." She jumped, snapping her blunt teeth, trying to break past the sheep. "If you had let us do what we wished w—"

"If I had let you do what you wished, Zoon would be burned to the ground!" Ironpaw leaped forward, sending the front sheep scurrying backward. His ears pointed straight up and his open mouth flexed like he might lunge to bite. Seeing the prowling wolf, the entire flock ran out of the pasture and surrounded Tully. The wolves edged toward the flock's flanks, nipping at the sheep's snouts, forcing them to cluster.

"Look around, you monster, you did burn it to the ground." Tully tried to push forward, but the flock continued to bunch tighter, slowly backing toward the fence.

"You did this, bah-bah, you and your stupid followers. You destroyed our free land." The sheep's rumps bumped into the fence. The wolves were five feet away.

"Enough!" Tweed broke his gaze from the office and jumped between the two tribes. "All of you stop right now." He

stood between Tully and Ironpaw, glancing from one to the
other. "There is more to this than any of us realized."

Ironpaw continued to snarl at Tully but watched Tweed.
"What do you mean more than we realized?"

Tweed turned back to the office as though he had not heard
him. Ironpaw glanced once more at the sheep and signaled for
the wolves to stand down. The sheep too dropped their guard.
The creatures watched in silence as Tweed walked toward the
door and gently knocked. "Chimp, I know you're in there. It's
time to let us inside."

Ironpaw walked up beside him and sniffed the door's thresh-
old. "Tweed, what do you mean more than we realized?"

"There's something here we failed to see." Tweed knocked
again. He stood on his hind legs and tried to look through the
peephole. "Chimp!"

Tully pressed her face through the iron bars, wiped away the
grime, and tried to see through the windows. "It doesn't look
like anyone is in there."

Tweed stepped back from the door. "He's in there. He's hesitant to come out. He has too much to lose."

"What do you mean?"

"Chimp! Today is not the day for your fancy words. Don't
lie and say the man is gone." Tweed pushed the creatures back
and examined the third-floor windows. "Chimp! I know you're
there. I'll give you ten seconds to open the door. Then we will
break it down. Don't test me, Chimp. It will be easy; Maximus
weakened it more than enough." Tweed motioned to Darkfang.
Twelve wolves lined up and readied to charge. "Ten! Nine!"

Inside the office a thick dust film coated the floor and walls.

The files on the desks had begun to yellow, and the coats in the closets were tattered with moth holes. Chimp sat atop a desk, trembling with his knees clutched to his chest. "Six! Five! Chimp, this is not a bluff. We will knock this door down." The ape scampered across the room and flung chairs and boxes, anything his hands could grab, behind the door. Outside, the wolves snorted like bulls and clawed the asphalt. "Three! Two! One!" Tweed moved away from the door. Snorting steam, the wolves barreled down the road and flung their full weight against the mutilated entrance. With a loud crash the office's steel barrier collapsed. Dust mushroomed into the air.

"Out of the way!" Ironpaw leaped over the pile of dazed wolves splayed on the crumpled door. Chimp swung wildly from the ceiling lights toward the back staircase, but Ironpaw tackled him and pinned the limp, helpless creature on the desk.

"Be gentle with him," nagged Tully, pressing into the room, shaking dust off her head. "You don't need to hurt him."

Tweed brushed past her. "Hold him still, Ironpaw. Don't let him run."

The ape squirmed under the wolf's paws, desperately trying to get free, but the more he wriggled, the harder Ironpaw's claws dug into his chest. "I have him. Why do you need him? What's going on, Tweed?"

"This ape has many things he needs to tell us." The interrogating panda stood on his hind legs beside the desk. He stroked the Chimp's face and whispered in his ear. "I have some questions for you. And I doubt you will enjoy them. Sit up." Ironpaw took his paws off the ape's chest. Chimp trembled but slowly sat up. His eyes darted from the staircase to Ironpaw and back to the staircase. Tweed wiped dust off the ape's quivering shoulders and sat him upright, legs hanging off the desk's edge. "You're nervous. You should be." Tweed suddenly slapped him across the face. "Look here, look at me. Ignore everyone else."

"Tweed, what on earth is going on?"

"Tully! Patience!" Tweed slapped him again. "Focus, Chimp. The questions I'm going to ask—will you give me truthful answers? You have lied a great deal. Will you tell me the truth?" The ape grimaced and massaged his face. Tweed raised his paw again.

"I'll tell you what I can."

"Good. That will do for now. Where is the zookeeper?"

"I…I…I don't know."

"We aren't accepting that answer anymore. You have lied to us too long. You said you would tell the truth." Tweed closed his eyes, then opened them. "Let us try again: Where is the zookeeper?"

The ape bit his lip and shook his head.

"This creature is useless," barked Ironpaw.

"He'll come around. Isn't that right, Chimp? You'll tell us what we need to know."

"He's like a limp fish."

"Shut your mouth and let Tweed do his work."

Tweed motioned for both of them to step back. "Space," he mouthed. "I need him alone." The twenty creatures inside the room stepped back ten feet but leaned in their ears. Having heard the ruckus of the previous five minutes, creatures throughout the land had begun to file into the road and approach the office. They lengthened necks and climbed into trees to peek through the windows. "Ah, much better, just you and me, Chimp. You can speak candidly now. Let us try once more: Where is the zookeeper?"

"Tweed, I tell you, I don't know."

"Then tell me what you do know."

"I know many things."

"I know you do, many more than I ever thought. That will come. For now, tell me, if you had to guess, where is the zookeeper?"

"He could be anywhere. He's hard to find. He is like...like...the wind. Sometimes he's here, other times not. Sometimes he's in the first room, other times the fourth, or no room at all. Often I forget he's here. He moves around quietly and rarely shows himself."

"Of course. And right now. Tell me, Chimp. Where is he right now?"

"I don't know."

"Chimp!" Tweed squeezed the ape's knee. "You're testing my patience. Do you know what happens when my patience reaches its end?" Chimp's eyes flashed at Ironpaw and the pack. "Ah, you do. I have never witnessed a creature eaten by hungry wolves, but I'm sure it's an unpleasant sight."

"Please," Chimp squealed. "I don't know. I don't know what to tell you. The pasture—check the pasture!"

Tweed glanced at Tully. "We just left there. The zookeeper isn't in the pasture."

"Not good enough, Chimp."

"Tweed, please, I swear to you I don't know."

"When did you last see the man?"

"I don't remember. It has been many days."

"If you begin another sentence with 'I don't' you will be wolf food. Do not test me. I am the only one protecting you. Why do you think it's so immensely difficult for you to remember anything about the zookeeper?"

"I don—I have been busy, busy tidying the office and keeping track of important matters."

"Tidying what office? This dust-filled hole? This place has been dirty for ten seasons. Chimp, are you telling the truth? Or are you lying through your rotting teeth?"

"The truth! I'm telling the truth. Don't hurt me." Chimp curled into the fetal position atop the desk.

Tweed grabbed the nape of Chimp's neck and jerked him upright. "Get up, you coward. Sit up." He smacked the withering creature across the face three times in rapid succession. "Tell us something or you're useless to me, and I'll throw your carcass in the road."

"There is nothing I can do. If I knew where he was, I would tell you; believe me more than anything I would tell. Oh, he can be a harsh man...so harsh. When he gets angry, and the—" Tweed slapped him again with his open paw. "Chimp, here, I am here. Pay attention to me."

"Tweed, he's stalling," said Ironpaw. "He's biding time."

"No he's not," said Tully. "He's scared and doesn't know what to do."

"I'll determine what he is and is not!" Tweed grabbed the ape's cheeks in his paws and stared into his eyes. His voice dropped below a whisper. "I won't tell them for you, Chimp. I want to hear the words from your mouth. Say it, Chimp, say the truth. Where is the zookeeper?"

"I don't know! For the love of everything in this land, how can I tell you about a man I haven't seen or heard!"

Tweed smirked. "There it is. You've never seen or heard the zookeeper?"

"What? No. I meant I haven't seen or heard him in a long time."

Tweed lunged across the table and socked the ape on the bridge of his nose. "You liar! You've tricked us all!"

Chimp clutched his broken nose blubbering as blood poured through his hands. "It was a mistake! The nervousness!"

"You've deceived everyone!" Tweed lifted his paw to swing again, but Tully and Ironpaw leaped on his back. "Get off me. You blind fools, get your filthy bodies off me." Tweed flung them to the ground and faced the hundreds of creatures in the road. "The reason Chimp can't answer our questions, the reason he's never seen the zookeeper is because the man doesn't exist!"

A hush fell over the creatures. Tully and Ironpaw froze on the ground. "There is no zookeeper!" bellowed Tweed. "He has never been here. This zoo has been alone since the beginning. We are the scribes of our own destinies, and we were led astray by this measly maggot."

"No!" wailed Chimp. "You have it wrong!"

"Don't lie to us!" roared Tweed. "You've done enough." Ironpaw leaped onto the desk and locked his jaws around the ape's throat. The creatures pressed against the windows, into the doorway and every possible crevice. The land fell silent as Tweed's voice echoed: "The reason I've been gone is because I searched for the zookeeper. After Maximus's death, I knew something was suspicious. I scoured the land. I shouted the man's name. I looked on the highest mountaintops and in the lowest valley floors. I pleaded for the zookeeper. And I never found him. That's when I realized the truth. The zookeeper is a figment of Chimp's imagination."

"No! You have it wrong!" vowed Chimp. "I didn't make the—" Ironpaw closed his jaws tighter around the ape's neck.

"I suspected it for years. The day the land was freed, Chimp realized the power he could possess. If he convinced us the zookeeper existed the masses would listen to him because creatures are that way. He laughed from the office while he watched the land implode into chaos. It was Chimp who attacked the innocent sheep; it was Chimp who brought the chest of beads; it was Chimp who murdered Maximus!"

"No! You don't understand." Chimp broke into a fit of tears. He kicked his legs and gasped for breath with the wolf's fangs around his throat. "I'm not a murderer. You're a liar. You were—" Ironpaw pressed his canines deeper into the throat.

"Maximus tried to break into the office because he had discovered Chimp's secret. Chimp was scared he would reveal the truth so he murdered him in his sleep. The next morning I went to inspect the body, and although no one had seen him in years, Chimp came to the cave to help me inspect. At first, I thought it was to protect the zookeeper. Now I see it was to protect himself. He tried to put me on a false trail, but that was his greatest mistake. I saw through his scheme the moment he walked into the cave."

Ironpaw swayed with the ape's neck in his jaws like he might shake at any moment and sever the spine. The wolf's eyes had narrowed to slits. Saliva moistened the beast's gums and started to trickle into the ape's fur. "But why, Chimp?" asked Tully. "Why would you do this to us?"

"Save your breath, Tully. He will lie to you too." Tweed glared menacingly at the ape. "He's an unmasked fraud, and nothing will save him now. Because of him, everything we have believed is a lie. Zoon Garden is not a paradise, it's a coward hiding behind a steel door."

Ironpaw squeezed so tightly that Chimp lurched to pry open the jaws. But he lacked the strength and became very quiet. It was hard to tell whether he had submitted to the charges, ceased his defense from exhaustion, or if he had lost consciousness.

"He deserves a traitor's death," growled Ironpaw through his clamped jowls on Chimp's windpipe. "I will kill him and eat him."

Tully shoved Tweed out of the way. "What's come over you? You can't eat a creature!"

"He deceived everyone and destroyed Zoon Garden. He deserves a torturous death."

"We don't eat our own kind."

Ironpaw dropped the unconscious ape on the desk. He licked his lips and a feral grin came over him. "He's not my kind. And neither are you." The wolf snarled and ripped a chunk of flesh from Chimp's leg.

"I said no!" Tully turned and donkey-kicked Ironpaw in the jaw. The wolf leaped on her and sunk his fangs into her snout. "Get off her!" Tweed cried. He tried to yank them apart. But in that one swift motion, the invisible flame of Zoon Garden, sparked to existence with the words "life, liberty, and happiness for all animals," reached the end of its fuse that had long been ready to detonate.

"Kill them all!" howled Darkfang. He leapt on Tully's flank. She kicked and moaned, but the pack swarmed her. They shredded her shoulders and gnawed her skull and tore flesh from bone. Snowy ran into the road, but the wolves chased her down. She screamed and screamed, and they ripped her apart.

The violence quickly spread through the interconnected zoo. Shrieks of agony filled the land as social restraints fell, and the beasts who had once been citizens tore each other limb from limb. Antelopes gored monkeys with their horns. Buffalos rammed wolves and flung them against fences. The sheep, known for their supposed loving and compassionate hearts, swarmed innocent creatures and with hard hooves clobbered their heads and kicked them on the ground.

With their long legs Isabella and Sharif stomped prairie dogs. Raka and Jonesy chased down capybaras and clawed them till blood flowed in the road. Eagle and Owl swooped down and gouged eyes and ears, blinding and deafening the beasts. They lifted small ones high in the sky and dropped them to their deaths. Pigeon flocks attacked from the tower and swarmed the two birds like fire ants, piling on their wings till they plummeted to the asphalt.

Tweed tried to run through the mayhem to the cave on the hill where, unbeknownst to the animals, he had been living since Maximus's death. But a serpent slithered into his path. The bear feigned left, then tried right, and then the snake sunk its fangs into his throat. Two tears of blood dripped from Tweed's esophagus, and he choked in the fetal position, holding his throat as black bile gurgled out of his mouth.

None expected to murder that day, few were aware of the savages inside them, but when the moment arrived, the land fell as quickly as it had arrived.

Hours later the majority of citizens lay dead in the road. The battle had slowed, but screams and moans of anguish echoed in the distance. Flies had begun to swarm the carcasses, and the smoke from a fire started in the mayhem rose into the sky. It billowed around the office and through the shattered windows.

Inside desks were upturned. Smashed ceiling tiles littered the floor. Chairs were fractured to tinder. Chimp peeked out from behind the coats in the closet and grabbed the blood-soaked rag tied around his bitten thigh. He had lost over a pint of blood and twice had nearly fainted, but he had cinched the cloth tighter and slowed the bleeding. It was hard through the haze, but on the road he saw masticated tendons, sightless eyes, pale bones poking through grizzled flesh, and pools of blood seeping into the asphalt's cracks. Coughing in fumes, he limped across the room to escape the smoke and clambered over the wreckage onto the staircase. Leaning against the rail, he circled upward one arduous step after another. On the second floor he passed a room with a made bed, dirty work boots against the wall and freshly pressed clothes hanging on a rack.

He hobbled higher and crawled onto the third floor. It was a single room, no more than twelve feet by twelve feet with a mahogany desk in the corner and a single straight-backed chair. Cluttered papers and letters covered the surface, and an un-capped black fountain pen rested on a stack of handwritten notes ready to be delivered. Scratched speedily in cursive hand, the ink still wet, they read:

MY FRIENDS, THE GREAT EXPERIMENT HAS
CONCLUDED.

Chimp hobbled to the desk. He strained to remember the
humans' language and frantically pressed the notes to his face.
But smoke was quickly rising up the stairs, engulfing the room
and stinging his eyes. He shook the notes, nearly crumpling
them in his hands. "What does it say? What does it bloody say?"
Coughing violently, groping for a way out, he dropped the notes
on the floor and stumbling across the room pushed open a small
door.

He tumbled onto the office's roof. The sky above was black
with smog. Multiple trees were burning as flames leapt through
the branches. Chimp beat the smog away with his hand and
stumbled across the hot shingles. Through the gap in the smoke
he saw a figure. It was about six feet tall on two legs with high
cheekbones and blue eyes. It stood silent and still at the roof's
edge, face somber, hands folded behind its back, observing the
carnage, the remnants of the garden. Had the man spoken,
Chimp would have struggled to understand him, but he kept
silent. He looked out on the bodies, the parts of bodies, the slabs
of unknown meat littered across the land, beads and decrees
abandoned alongside them. A sudden smirk ticked on the man's
lips. He smiled, and then the zookeeper threw his head back and
laughed at that great land called Zoon Garden.

Acknowledgements

I am indebted to the late masters, Orwell, Hemingway, and most notably Dostoevsky, who set a standard for which to strive, as well as to Steinbeck, Kafka, and Garcia-Marquez whose lives and sufferings motivated me beyond compare. I thank the doubters and the rejecters, for whom without I would never know the joys of a hard-trudged path.

To my childhood friends and family Chris, Ellen, Liam, Tom Jr., Tom III, and Elida your selflessness was beyond expression. Carmen and Rodney, I owe you more than a man can repay; your kindness was, and still is, unparalleled. Thank you always to my editors Dave Burton and Michael Coghlan whose expertise saved my flippant grammatical soul, and to Lisa Germano and Donnie Etz whose pro bono work brought this project to fruition. Jake, Alan, and our band of misfits, the highest praise is reserved for you. Thank you for your relentless belief in a vision few others saw.

About the Author

Jordan O'Donnell is a novelist, businessman, adventurer, and a guy who likes to have a good time. Together with his tour manager, Jake Harris, he quit his job at the FBI, built a farmhouse, converted a 1993 International school bus into a solar-powered skoolie, bought two travel trailers, recruited 18 interns and embarked on a cross-country promotion tour.

A fan of fellow humans, Jordan encourages you to contact him. He would be happy to start a conversation about anything under the sun. Do note he lives on a bus in the woods and is liable at any moment to throw his phone down a well so please forgive any delayed responses.

You can learn more about the trip, the book, the author, and perhaps a bit about life at:

www.jordanodonnellauthor.com
Facebook.com/JordanODonnellAuthor
Twitter and Instagram: @jordanodonnellauthor

If you are interested in learning about the novel's meaning or allegorical interpretations visit: Goodreads, Librarything, Reddit, or any other online discussion board.

CPSIA information can be obtained
at www.ICGtesting.com
Printed in the USA
LVHW091924130620
658000LV00010B/490